SNAKE POINT

JAMES N. BADE

World Castle Publishing, LLC
Pensacola, Florida
Copyright © James N. Bade 2021
Paperback ISBN: 9781955086400
eBook ISBN: 9781955086417
First Edition World Castle Publishing, LLC, July 12, 2021
http://www.worldcastlepublishing.com
Licensing Notes
Cover: Karen Fuller
Editor: Maxine Bringenberg

CHAPTER 1

"This must be the bumpiest road in Germany!" said Tom. "We've got potholes in New Zealand, but nothing like this. Surely there must be some other way to get to the CNN people at Lake Stechlin."

"There doesn't seem to be," Luise replied. "Bus 836 is the way to get there from Gransee Station."

"I didn't mind the RE5 train ride, Luise, but this is ridiculous!"

"Well, it's not as bad as the road to the Potsdam wrestling meet I went to last night," Jake commented, as the bus took a sudden lurch to the right to avoid a pothole. "That must be the bumpiest concrete road in Europe. When you're standing on the sidewalk at Schilfhof, the traffic sounds like horses galloping past!"

"How did the wrestling go last night?" Tom asked.

"Good! It was Potsdam versus Artern. Lots of

students from Potsdam University. But when I got there, two of the Potsdam wrestlers had to withdraw because of injury—86 and 66 kg. I offered to step in for the 86 kg guy. And won! That gave Potsdam four points they would have lost otherwise. So they won the dual!"

"Boy, I bet they were pleased!"

"They sure were, Tom! They took me off to celebrate afterwards in a place called *Full House*—probably named after the TV show—but it wasn't a full house, we were the only people there. I told them I couldn't stay long, though, with this CNN interview coming up this morning."

"Has your wrestling season finished at Oklahoma, Jake?" Luise asked.

"We're halfway through. We've got a bit of a break now. Our fall term finished last week, and the spring term starts mid-January. Actually, I'd just gotten back from the last wrestling dual of the season, against the University of Pittsburgh, when I got your message about the CNN news team wanting to interview us. How did they find out about us?"

"Apparently, Judy Thorpe alerted them. They wanted to know where we should meet. I thought of Lake Stechlin because that's the area everyone associates with Fontane. Seeing I knew Tom was on a study abroad course in Zürich, I thought he could get to Berlin quite easily. I just wasn't sure if you could."

"Just the right time of the year for me. That's why I jumped at the chance! How's Zürich, Tom?"

"I really like it there. I got a room in a student hostel at Freudenbergstrasse. Lovely view of the city, when you can see it — the fog has rolled in now from the lake, and it's getting a lot colder. But the university is great. It's got a Lichthof just like the one at the Technical University in Berlin — you know, a huge indoor atrium with a big glass dome — and it's got a statue of Nike in it too!"

"Is the statue anything like the Berlin one?" asked Luise.

"Almost exactly the same, on a big black stone pedestal that says the statue dates back to two centuries B.C. Have a look!"

Tom showed them photos of the Nike statue that he had taken on his phone.

"Oh, very nice! I like the pink background," commented Luise.

"Yes, but the statue's not illuminated like the Berlin one," said Tom.

"How does your course fit in with your cricket, Tom?" asked Jake.

"Well, it meant I was in the first two matches, but then I had to miss the rest of the first half of the season. The study abroad course is a three-week advanced German language course, so it's not too long, and it's just finished, so I'll be back for the start of the second half of the season in January."

"Any more centuries?"

"Ha ha! No! Got thirty-six runs in my last game, though! Hey, Luise, how did you manage to get time off for the interview?"

"Well, I haven't got any lectures today. We finish for the year at the end of this week, then start again towards mid-January."

"So you're making the most of it, then!"

"*Aber natürlich*! But of course! Look, we're just arriving at Neuglobsow. We have to get out here. From here, we can walk down to the lake."

Tom and Jake got out of the bus while Luise asked the driver about buses back to Gransee later in the day so they could get back to Berlin in the afternoon. Tom and Jake looked at the surroundings. There were still signs of late autumn colors on the trees, which lined a narrow cobbled lane sprinkled with leaves, wending its way past a number of unpretentious houses and buildings. To their right was a grassy slope down to the water.

"Not much to see here," Jake commented. "Is that the lake over there?"

"If it is, it's pretty small," said Tom.

"No, that's Lake Dagow," said Luise, who had now joined them. "It's just a little one. Lake Stechlin is the main lake here. It's down this way, about twenty minutes' walk down the road, past the museum on the right. We've arranged to meet the CNN people at eleven, so we've got about half an hour."

They set out down the lane, passing a number of Tudor-style buildings on the left and a modern green building on the right, which turned out to be the museum.

"I imagine this is a pretty popular place in the summer, judging from all the parks and benches and bike stands everywhere. What's this village called again?" Tom asked.

"Neuglobsow," Luise replied.

"What a funny name!" Jake laughed.

"Well, funnily enough, Fontane's novel is set here, and Fontane stayed here, but Neuglobsow never appears in the novel at all. Instead, he set his novel in a village called Stechlin, named after the lake. You know how we said Fontane had an uncanny way of foretelling the future? Well, in his day, there was no locality called Stechlin. But now this whole area is called the Municipality of Stechlin."

"Is that because of his novel?" Jake asked.

"Largely, yes. Stechlin is one of his best known novels. It's a plea for tolerance and open-mindedness and getting rid of the parochialism and insularity Fontane saw in Germany at the time. People identified with it."

"So Fontane put Stechlin on the map."

"Yes, you could say that, Jake. And when

people think of Stechlin, they think of Fontane. That's why I think it's a good idea to meet the CNN people at Lake Stechlin."

"And is that Fontane Street I can see coming up on the left?" asked Tom.

"Well, yes, there has to be a Fontane Street here, doesn't there? Now, see that little Tudor-style building coming up on the left? That's where Fontane stayed. It's now called the Fontane House—it's a restaurant. And that tree there is the one that Fontane sat under."

"Ah yes, it's got a sign on it," said Jake. "And I reckon this is one even I can translate. You betcha! Under this tree sat Theodor Fontane!"

The others laughed.

"And I bet all the restaurant dishes are named after Fontane," commented Tom.

"Yes, they are, I think. But I can do one better than that. Lake Stechlin has a species of fish not found anywhere else in the world, and it's named after Fontane. Coregonus fontanae. A type of salmon."

"So we could eat Fontane for breakfast," Tom grinned.

"Well, in theory, yes, but they say they're very small. Shows you how special Lake Stechlin is, though. Quite unique. They have set up a research station devoted to water ecology and freshwater fishing to investigate it. There's a raft on the lake taking measurements all the time. There's also a meteorological station there run by the Ministry for the Environment, looking at the impact of climate change. All run on solar energy, too."

"Climate change, eh? That's a really important question for our generation. And what's that big house on the left?" asked Jake.

On the other side of a large wrought iron fence, they could see a tall turreted white Tudor-style mansion nestled at the back of a huge garden, with a grand concrete staircase leading up to it.

"Ah, yes! Lots of people that come here after reading Fontane's novel think this must be his Stechlin Castle. But it wasn't actually built till the 1930s. Like the village of Stechlin, it didn't exist in Fontane's day. It was a product of his imagination."

"Artistic license, then?" asked Tom.

"Yes, but it exists now, just as his Stechlin exists now too! But this building here is something that's very close to my heart. It's the yoga house. They have yoga retreats here. My yoga friends in Berlin love coming here."

They took a selfie of the three of them in front of the yoga house and admired the "Yoga Haus" inscription on the glass doors before moving on down the road and into the forest, where the road narrowed down to a paved track. They passed two men in business suits chatting in the parking lot at the entrance to the forest and followed the track through the trees. These had lost most of their leaves, but there was still a colorful mixture of light green, yellow, and orange to be seen on the trees, and the ground on both sides of the track was covered with a thick layer of brown leaves.

"You know, I'm sure we've seen those men before," Jake commented after a while.

"Yes, I thought they looked familiar too," said Tom. "Especially the one with the pasty face and glasses. I'm sure we've seen the guy with the beard too. But I can't remember where."

"Well, who knows, they might have something to do with CNN," said Luise. "I've arranged to meet the CNN team just a bit further down the track on the right. There's a large circular seating arrangement there, so they'll have plenty of room for their equipment."

Sure enough, as they came towards the end of the track and the lake started to open up in front of them, they could see a group of people with microphones and camera equipment set up in the picnic area. As they approached, a young woman waved to them and came out onto the track.

"Aha! The Glass Mountains team! I recognized you immediately from Judy Thorpe's description—she called you the Glass Mountains Mission. Hi, I'm Helen Harlowe—I'll be interviewing you. And this is my team; Patrick McBryde, who is overseeing the whole operation; Christine Niven, in charge of microphones and sound; Brian Duncan, the cameraman; and Keith Leighton, looking after the drone."

Luise, Jake, and Tom shook hands with the CNN crew.

"I'm actually an auto mechanic by trade," said Brian. "But now I drive the cameras. Not too much difference, really. Always breaking down and needing replacement parts."

"And I drive the drone," grinned Keith. "That's where Brian's knowledge really comes in useful. They are always crashing and needing repair."

"And we're always having problems with the microphones as well," Christine sighed.

"Well, I'm sure that will fill them all with the greatest of confidence," laughed Patrick. Somehow the general laughter helped everyone relax.

"Let's move down to the lake," said Keith, "and if I can get the drone to behave, I'll get a drone shot of you three shaking hands with Helen at the lakeside. That way, we can get the natural beauty of the lake and forest right at the very beginning."

They walked down to the lake, and while Keith's drone buzzed around above, Helen stood at the shore of the lake greeting and shaking hands with the trio. At Patrick's suggestion, they re-enacted the meeting twice more, so it could be captured from three different angles.

"Not often we shake hands with the same person three times in a row," Tom laughed.

"No, we do it quite often, though," said Helen. "Viewers don't often realize all the work that goes into these seemingly chance encounters."

Brian and Christine then moved up to the group. Brian set up the camera while Christine attached tiny microphones to the jackets of the trio and put on her headphones.

"Now, just say anything to anyone, and I'll make sure they're working. I should be able to hear everything you say. Ah, perfect. Just remember to take them off before you go to the toilet. There have been embarrassing situations in the past."

They all chuckled at this and waited while Helen retrieved her notes from Patrick.

"All righty. First question. Tell us about the Glass Mountains Mission. How did you get together, and what's it all about?"

CHAPTER 2

"Who would like to go first?"

Luise explained how Judy Thorpe, the United Nations Special Envoy for Conflict Resolution, had set up a special mission to investigate a mysterious sketch found in the Fontane Archives in Potsdam, which claimed to have vital information for the future of mankind. Through her friend Professor Aurisch, at the University of Auckland in New Zealand, and his contacts, the three of them had been chosen on the strength of their academic knowledge and personalities to investigate this sketch.

Jake then talked about his Oklahoman Mennonite background and how he had recognized the sketch as a map of the Glass Mountains in Oklahoma, near the Mennonite community where Fontane had set his anti-war novel *Quitt*.

Tom spoke about the mysterious times and dates given on the sketch and how he had worked out that in 1891 the people must have calculated that the next time the summer solstice would occur over the Glass Mountains at the same time as in 1891 would be in 2019—coincidentally, the two-hundredth anniversary of Fontane's birth. So the sun would be in exactly the same position on June 21, 2019, and the instruction was to stand on Cathedral Mountain at the time of the summer solstice and see what happened.

Jake then described how the sun reflected from five different points at the moment of the full solstice, merging on a particular spot, and at that spot, they had dug up an old nickel tobacco box. A document inside it referred to the message of Obadja's sermon in Fontane's novel and its importance for the future of humanity. And that message was that if mankind is to survive, we must get beyond the revenge mentality.

Luise clarified that Fontane was concerned about the escalation of the arms race towards the end of the nineteenth century. International rivalry was so bad that war could break out for any reason, and he knew that such a war would be disastrous. His idea was to get rid of that revenge mentality, so there would be no need for war. There must be some other way to resolve differences.

"But why did he think people might appreciate that more by 2019?" Helen asked.

"Well, *Quitt* is a strongly anti-war novel," said Tom. "But Europe was gearing up for war, and he realized that hardly anyone would be listening. He must have felt that by 2019, two-hundred years after his birth, his message would have more of a chance of getting through."

At this point, Patrick indicated that he would like a word with Helen. After consulting for several minutes, they turned to Jake, Luise, and Tom.

"That was an excellent interview, thank you very much," Patrick told the trio. "We'd now like to have a chat with Judy Thorpe in New York about her thoughts, and we'd like to meet up with you again in a couple of weeks at the Glass Mountains. Would that be possible? If so, what we'd like you to do, if it's at all feasible, is to come up with a manifesto for your special mission. I realize you will need a bit of time to write a manifesto, but we could launch it on the Glass Mountains in early January. That would give you a lot of publicity."

"And what exactly do you mean by a manifesto?" asked Jake.

"A manifesto is a public declaration of your views. A summary that people can identify with. It might take you a few days to write, but it would be well worthwhile."

"Well, I've got my Freie Universität Berlin Christmas break coming up, so time-wise there's no problem for me," said Luise. "Would you be able to drive us around Oklahoma again, Jake?"

"My University of Oklahoma spring term doesn't start till January twelfth, so I've got time, and I could certainly drive the three of us to the Glass Mountains for an interview. How about you, Tom?"

"Semester one at the University of Auckland doesn't start till the end of February, so I've got plenty of time, and I could fly back via Oklahoma. The only thing that worries me is how we would pay for the air fares. Do you think they might have money in the UN Special Envoy budget?"

"Well, we can only ask," said Jake, and turning to Patrick, added, "Looks like we'll be able to get to the Glass Mountains whenever you can make it."

"If we've got funding to cover it, I'll be there," said Tom. "And I can see you'll be there too, Luise?"

Luise nodded.

"Excellent!" said Patrick. "Now, as far as I'm concerned, this interview is over, and we'll certainly be covering it in our news, but we'll meet up again for the launch of your manifesto at the Glass Mountains in a couple of weeks' time. Where are you three off to now? Berlin?"

"No, we're off on a walk around the lake first. There's so much mythology associated with this area and so much to explore."

"Great! I'll get Keith to get a drone shot of you heading down the lake track. Then we can get another shot of the lake and the forest. It's just so calm and peaceful here, with lovely scenery. The lake is like a mirror, lined with beautiful late autumn colors."

"Does that mean we have to do this one over three times as well?" asked Tom.

Everyone laughed, and they all shook hands and exchanged thanks as Christine and Brian packed the camera and sound gear away, and Keith sent the drone up over the lake, with Patrick carefully monitoring the image.

"Take care," said Helen as the trio moved off down the track alongside the lake.

"See you on the Glass Mountains," Jake called out as they all waved goodbye.

On their way down the track through the forest that bordered the lake, Jake asked, "All round the jetty back there, there are these huge metallic red roosters. Why's that? What's the significance?"

"You're right—the red rooster is identified with Lake Stechlin. It's part of the local mythology," said Luise.

"Yes, I seem to remember Fontane mentions it right at the beginning of his novel," Tom remarked.

"Absolutely, along with a number of other things—we'll get on to those in a minute," Luise commented. "The story goes that when something important is going on in the outside world that people need to know about, a huge red rooster appears out of the depths and crows out such a loud warning it can be heard some distance away."

"And how did this myth originate?"

"Well, Jake, according to legend, a fisherman gathering in his net during a storm on the lake was confronted by a red rooster, which rose out of the water and dragged him into the depths."

"And is there any scientific explanation for this?"

"Well, because of the storm, some people have explained it as a waterspout catching the rays of the sinking sun. But there is another theory, and that is that the lake is volcanic, and what happened is that some methane gas bubbled up to the surface and was ignited by the fisherman's torch."

"Is there any truth behind that theory?"

"Well, there is tectonic evidence that the lake did respond to the big Lisbon earthquake of 1755. The Stechlin is one of the deepest lakes in Europe."

"And that's the reason why Fontane characterized the lake as keeping the local population in touch with distant events?" said Tom. "For me, the lake is the main character in the novel. It's always warning the characters not to be too complacent, not to isolate themselves from the rest of the world, to constantly be on their guard against forces which may be conspiring against them."

At this point, they spied a wooden bench overlooking the lake and decided to sit down and see what they could observe. The bench was about a meter from the shore. With a slight wind coming up, the water was gently lapping up against the bank below them. To their left and right were a number of trees leaning over the edge of the lake into the water, and in some cases, the branches were submerged. The ground was covered with reddish-yellow leaves. Closer to the lake, the green of the moss-covered bank teamed nicely with the light green of the few leaves still remaining on the smaller shrubs growing on the bank.

"I can see that if you sat here long enough, you might imagine you've seen something," remarked Jake. "What's that white thing over there, Luise, floating on the lake?"

"That's the research station raft I was telling you about. It's constantly taking samples of the lake water."

"I see. But hang on, I think I can see something else." Tom pointed out at the surface of the lake. "Look over there, about ten meters out from the shore. Isn't that something coming out of the lake?"

They stared intently at the area Tom was pointing at. Sure enough, there seemed to be something emerging from the lake. A creature of some sort?

"Looks like a rhinoceros's head," said Tom. "What is it?"

"I reckon it's the tip of a large tree trunk that's

been buried in the lake," Jake suggested. "It's the water lapping up and down that makes it look like it's emerging. If you look closely, you can see it's not actually moving."

They looked carefully and decided Jake was right.

"Just shows you, if you look long enough, you'll find something," Tom remarked. "I think it's all psychological."

At that, the trio decided to move further down the track around the lake. After a while, a wooden trellis fence appeared on the right, and then some buildings became visible through the trees. As they walked further, they came across an open space full of what looked like rain gauges, and there was a large building with a roof completely covered with solar panels.

"Is this the meteorological station you were telling us about?" Jake asked.

"Yes, there's a sign down here about it," said Luise.

They gathered around the sign explaining how the station took meteorological readings of temperature, wind direction and speed, rainfall, and air pollution, recording the effect of climate change on the environment.

"Sweet as!" said Tom. "Sounds like they are taking climate change seriously here at least."

"Well, yes, they are," Luise sighed. "But you know, I think they're trying to make up for what used to go on here."

"What do you mean by that?"

"Well, believe it or not, they used to have a nuclear power station at Lake Stechlin."

Jake looked incredulous. "What?! But I thought this was supposed to be a conservation area. A state park, like the Glass Mountains. I read somewhere it had been a state park since 1938."

"Yes, that's true. But the East German government found an area right on the lake that was exempt. The Nazis had used it as a hunting lodge. So in their wisdom, the East German government built a nuclear power station there. And used water from the lake to cool it. That meant the lake was nice and warm around the power station, so people came from miles around to go swimming there at all times of the year. It was very popular!"

"Good grief! That must have increased the temperature of the lake by several degrees."

"Yes, it did, Tom."

"Talk about climate change! I see what you mean about trying to make up for it. Mind you, we can't talk," said Jake. "There are some parts of the Pacific where people still can't live because of our nuclear testing. You're lucky New Zealand is nuclear-free, Tom."

"Yes, that's right. But everyone is affected by climate change, New Zealand included," Tom commented.

They now followed the paved track as it left the research institute behind and re-entered the forest. The colors changed from the green of the open spaces to the orange, dark red, and yellow of the forest as they made their way along the track covered with dark red leaves. On both sides were large trees which had lost their leaves and smaller shrubs which still had leaves on them of varying hues of yellow, light green, and brown. The lake was still visible, though, through the trunks of the deciduous trees.

About ten minutes' walk past the research institute, Luise pointed to a clearing at the side of the lake. She explained that in the winter excursion in the novel, Dubslav took his party to this point, where, according to legend, the lake was supposed to have erupted at certain key points in history.

"Let's sit down here," she said. "All sorts of unusual phenomena have been observed in this part of the lake. This is where, in the novel, Melusine is convinced there is something lurking in the depths of the lake and thinks a hand will come out and drag her under. Anything can happen here."

CHAPTER 3

From the clearing, they had an unobstructed view across the lake to the hills on the other side, which were basking in the early winter sunshine, displaying a delicate reddish shade from the leaves still on the trees. On the left was a dark green peninsula jutting into the lake, and between the peninsula and the shore on which they were now sitting was clear water, reflecting the light blue sky. It was very quiet; the only thing to be heard was the sound of the water lapping against the shore. As they looked around at the dark red blanket of leaves on the ground and the contrast with the light yellow color of the younger shrubs and the green of the reeds growing along the shoreline, they were amazed at the large number of fallen trees.

"It's pretty calm at the moment, but my guess is that it can get really gusty here — look at all those trees that have been uprooted," Tom remarked. "I wonder if that accounts for all these legends. Mini tornadoes, water spouts?"

"Well, this is where all the mysterious events are supposed to have happened," said Luise. "Responding to incidents all round the world, so they say. In the first page of his *Stechlin* novel, Fontane says how quiet it can be around the lake, yet at this particular point, there can be a sudden disturbance, a reaction to a volcanic event elsewhere in the world — a water spout usually, but sometimes instead of the water spout the red rooster appears, screeching out its warning."

"What sort of volcanic events?" Jake asked.

"Well, he says it might be in Iceland or Java, or even a Hawaiian volcano sending its clouds of ash way out over the South Pacific."

"Mt. Kilauea in Hawaii is the biggest active volcano in the U.S.," said Jake. "I remember reading about that in geography. And last year when it erupted, it sent an ash cloud all the way over to the Mariana Islands to the southwest, nearly four-thousand miles away."

"Well, that puts it within the range of New Zealand because Tokelau is part of New Zealand and is just over two thousand miles to the southwest of Hawaii," said Tom, reading from his phone. "Tokelau is New Zealand's northernmost territory. Our prime minister visited there earlier this year."

"But would it have gone that far south?"

"Well, my friends in Aitutaki told me that in the 1960s, the British were still measuring atmospheric radiation levels there from their nuclear testing at Christmas Island ten years earlier. According to this website, Aitutaki is fifteen-hundred miles due south of Christmas Island, so yes, prevailing winds would take ash clouds that way."

"How amazing that this lake right in the middle of Brandenburg could be connected somehow to the South Pacific," mused Luise. "Well, let's watch it for a while and see if anything happens."

"Gee, I would have thought if there is anything to be observed, the research station here would have noticed it," said Jake.

Tom looked out at the lake intently. "I reckon we should stay here for a few minutes. If this is where Dubslav brings them in the novel, then this is an important spot for the mythology of the area, if nothing else."

"Alrighty, I'm with you, Tom. Strange how quiet it is here. No bird life either from the sound of things."

"Just a few insects around. Mainly dragonflies. Too late in the year for bees," Luise commented.

As they sat there, though, they became aware of a loud buzzing noise, and they looked around to see where it was coming from.

"I've heard of bees swarming, but dragonflies?" said Jake. "Where are they all? I can only see a few on the water."

They looked up and could see a big cloud of dragonflies above them.

"We get swarms of dragonflies back home, too," said Jake.

"What on earth are they doing here?" asked Tom.

The buzzing from the dragonflies got louder and louder until they could hardly stand it anymore. Then suddenly, out of nowhere, there was a huge clap of thunder, which resonated across the water and came back as a muffled echo from the bays opposite.

"*Mein Gott!*" Luise gasped. "I've never heard thunder like that before!"

"That was thunder all right," said Jake. "But I didn't see any lightning, did you? Where did it come from?"

"Hang on! Look over there!" Tom pointed towards the peninsula on the other side of the lake. "About thirty meters out that way. Isn't that something coming out of the lake?"

"Wow!" Jake looked in the direction Tom was pointing. "There looks to be something out there all right."

"And listen," said Luise. "The buzzing has stopped. The dragonflies have gone."

They looked around. Sure enough, the dragonflies were nowhere to be seen. All three then gazed intently at the spot on the lake where something seemed to be emerging.

"If this is any sort of eruption, we need to keep well clear," said Tom. "We had an eruption in New Zealand on White Island just last week, and twenty-one people got killed. The sulfurous fumes are deadly. At least here, we can escape if we run fast enough. White Island is so small you haven't got a chance."

The trio moved back to the track so they could make a wild dash for it if necessary but stood there absolutely enthralled by the spectacle unfolding before them. The object seemingly emerging from the water turned out to be a kind of waterspout, which slowly rose out of the lake. It was a clear column of sparkling water, which rose straight up into the air and sprinkled the surface of the lake immediately around it with delicate droplets of water.

"I wonder what that is? The water doesn't look hot, there's no steam — it's not a geyser," said Tom.

Then as they watched, the vertical shaft of water slowly rose further, and at its base, the clear water appeared to have turned a light reddish-brown color, matching the color of the leaves that covered the bank.

"What's causing that? Is it the leaves from the trees that have sunk to the bottom of the lake?" Jake asked.

"But if it was leaves, we'd be able to see them," Luise remarked. "This is still clear water. It's as if the water spout has been illuminated from underneath by beams of light."

As they watched, the color slowly crept up the column of water until it was completely red.

"This must be the red rooster, then!" Tom gulped. "This is the red fountain of water which sounds its warning to those that see it. And yet it's not making any noise at all."

Tom was right. It was completely still—there was no noise to be heard anywhere. The buzzing of the insects, which had been so deafening just a few minutes ago, had given way to complete silence. If they listened very carefully, they could hear the sound of the fountain of water pattering down on the surface of the lake around it, which was completely motionless. But that was the only sound. Apart from that, you could have heard a pin drop. They all got out their phones and started taking photos and videos of the extraordinary phenomenon they were witnessing.

"To me, this is a miniature of what happens on Mt. Kilauea," Jake commented. "A Mt. Kilauea eruption is quite distinctive. From photos I've seen, the red lava fountains in a narrow column straight into the sky just like this—they call it vertical jetting. With other volcanoes, the lava goes in all directions."

"And yet this version doesn't look dangerous," said Luise. "It looks somehow welcoming. It's almost as if it's inviting us over there. Don't worry, I'm not suggesting we head over there. But it looks like a friendly presence. If it's warning us about something, it seems to be somehow well disposed towards us."

Then as they watched, the reddish-brown color started to fade, and the column of water turned clear again. The waterspout began to retract as if the vertical pillar of water was lowering itself back into the lake. And as it returned to the lake, the eerie silence abated, the ripples returned to the surface of the water, and the reassuring sound of the waves lapping against the shore returned. Then, just as the trio heaved a collective sigh of relief that things were returning to normal, the buzzing sound that they had heard earlier started up again, but this time it seemed to be coming from out on the lake, in the direction of the peninsula.

"What's that?" Jake pointed to what seemed to be a cloud of insects hovering above the lake. Then as they watched, the cloud started moving towards them.

They took out their phones to take photos and videos as the swarm approached. The buzzing noise slowly grew until it again became utterly deafening. Then some of the dragonflies started to depart from the dense insect cloud above them and headed out over the lake, followed by the others, so that eventually a long line of dragonflies extended from where they were standing to halfway across the lake.

"You know what this is?" Tom called out to the others. "It's the Atafu omen!"

"An omen? What do you mean?"

"This is exactly what happened at Atafu in Tokelau, Jake."

"You mean the New Zealand territory you were talking about before? That would have gotten ash from Mt. Kilauea in Hawaii?"

"Yes, that's it. I was reading about it the other day. It happened in 1845. The dragonflies that had been circling around the village proceeded in a line out to sea and disappeared into the ocean. The Tokelauans said they represented evil spirits. It was called the Atafu omen."

"But these aren't disappearing into the distance," Luise observed. "They're in a straight line all right, but they seem to be heading for the wharf, where we came from."

"Where the red roosters are? Well, let's make sure we've got a decent record of these things," said Tom. "We might be the only people that have ever taken photos or videos of these. You can see why there is so much mythology associated with this lake."

They decided to take several selfies with the mysterious line of insects behind them extending out into the lake. Then Luise reminded them that there were only two more buses back to Gransee that afternoon, so they had better start heading back.

They walked back exactly the way they had come, following the leaf-covered track through the forest, through the clearing, along the cobbled road past the research center buildings and meteorological station on the left, back into the forest track, and alongside the edge of the lake past the boat hire station. They stopped to look at all the boats neatly piled up, Luise explaining that in the summer, the jetty was packed with people taking boats out, rowing boats and kayaks and that some even spent the whole day on the lake. Jake had just commented that they should come back in the summer and do just that when he noticed something unusual.

"Look over there." He pointed to the end of the jetty. "Those two guys. Aren't they the same guys we saw earlier, and we thought we'd seen them somewhere before?"

"Oh yes!" said Tom. "We saw them back at the car park. Pasty Face and Beardy Weirdy! I wonder what they're doing there."

They were just heading out of the forest towards the jetty when the two men walked onto the track and, as the three approached, blocked their way.

Luise looked at them sternly. "*Mein Gott! Was machen Sie denn*? What do you think you're doing?"

"We've been waiting for you," said the man

with the beard. "We need to warn you that you are in dangerous territory."

"Dangerous territory! What do you mean? You can't just block us like this!" said Tom.

"Oh, yes we can," said the pasty-faced man with glasses. "And in more ways than one. We know all about you."

CHAPTER 4

"What do you mean, you know all about us?" Luise challenged the two men.

"We know where you live in Corn, Oklahoma, Jake — we know exactly where your study is and what you've got in it. And we've got all the information you had on your laptop," said the man with the beard.

"My laptop?" cried Jake. And then he remembered last year's break-in of his study, for which local criminal Kobe Wight had been arrested. "You mean to say that Kobe Wight wasn't working alone when he broke into my study?"

"Well, put it this way — he's not as dumb as he looks. He passed on all that information he found on the laptop to us. We've been following your activities ever since. We know all about you, and we know all about Luise and Tom as well."

"So it was you two that we saw outside the United Nations building in New York?" Tom asked.

"We thought we recognized you!"

"Yes, that was us," said the man with the pasty face. Turning to all three, he declared with some severity, "That CNN interview was the last straw. We have to stop you now."

"We will stop you at every opportunity," said his bearded companion. "We will block you at every highway and byway. If you don't stop your nonsense, we will find a way to end it."

"How dare you talk to us like that!" said Tom, moving right up to the bearded stranger and staring him straight in the eye.

"You keep away from me, or you'll regret it," said the stranger, raising his fist.

"*Nein, nein!*" shouted Luise, pushing her way between the two and trying to keep them apart.

Suddenly the bearded stranger violently pushed her away, thumping her in the shoulder, sending her reeling backwards into a tree. She grabbed her shoulder, screaming in agony. The stranger then gripped Tom by his shirt while his companion raised his fist to deal with Jake, who had now intervened between Tom and his assailant.

"Watch it. You're dealing with a wrestling champion here," said Jake. "I can make mincemeat out of both of you."

At this, both men stepped back. Tom was comforting Luise, who was in a lot of pain.

"*Polizei*! Call the police!" she was shrieking.

"Police! You just go ahead and try! We have ways of dealing with people like you," said the pasty-faced man. "We are warning you. We'll let you pass now, but if you continue, we will stop you in your tracks."

The men stood aside, and the trio walked on, shaken. Luise was clutching her shoulder in such pain that she was gasping with agony.

"I reckon you've dislocated your shoulder, Luise," said Jake. "That happened to me once in the middle of a wrestling match. You need to put your arm in a sling. Anything will do. How about this jersey of mine?"

Jake took off his jersey and tied it around Luise's neck as a sling to support her arm, and they emerged from the forest. They were just starting to walk up the road that led to the bus stop when Jake suddenly caught sight of the CNN van parked outside the Fontane house on the right.

He ran up to the CNN van and saw that the hood was up and Brian was inspecting the engine. The others were sitting on some seats under Fontane's tree.

He leapt over the small fence separating the seating area from the road, ran up to them, and told them about what had happened. He asked them if they might have any ice for Luise's shoulder.

Helen jumped up and had a look at the back of the van. "Let's see what we've got in our ice box. How about a packet of frozen peas? I remember that helped me a lot when I sprained my wrist once."

She guided Luise to her seat and gave her the frozen peas, showing exactly how she needed to apply them to the painful area. Luise felt some relief already.

"You must make sure you seek medical help, though," said Patrick. "You need to apply something cold to relieve the pain, but if it's a dislocated shoulder, a doctor might be able to put it back in position. I wish we could take you to a medical center ourselves, but our van has an overheating problem. Brian's just looking to see what's causing it. Terrible smell!"

"That's all right. As long as we get the connections to Berlin, I can get to the medical center at Rüdersheimer Platz, close to where we are staying," said Luise, feeling her pain was much more under control.

"Enjoy Fontane's linden tree in the meantime," Helen suggested. "I've always liked linden trees. Lovely colors in the fall. It's shed most of its leaves, but I love the bright yellow of the leaves that are left. I can see why Fontane enjoyed sitting here. But listen, tell us about these two men that blocked your way and then assaulted you. That is shocking behavior. I think we should call the police."

Patrick thought for a while. "They must have been listening to the interview. We get all sorts of weirdos hanging around when we do our interviews. You'll probably never see them again, but if they do cause any trouble, we're happy to help in whatever way we can. We've been in situations like this before. We could suggest a plan of action. I guess the most obvious thing to do is go to a place where they could never find you. Easier said than done, of course."

There was a long silence, broken by Christine, who asked, "Hey listen, how did you guys get on before these men turned up?"

Luise, Jake and Tom then proceeded to tell them in great detail about what they had seen, particularly the red column of water that had arisen out of the lake.

"It looked like a miniature eruption," Jake told them. "Vertical jetting like Mt. Kilauea."

Keith said he had helped cover the 2018 Mt. Kilauea eruption for CNN. His drone had enabled him to get some quite dramatic shots. "How far along the lake did you see it?" Keith asked. "I might have enough time to get there and back by the time the van is fixed. What do you reckon, Brian?"

Brian poked his head out from under the hood. "Looks like the ventilation radiator has developed a coolant leak," he said. "We won't be able to fix this in a hurry. Might have to get alternative transport. Whatever we do, it'll take over an hour, so if you want to go down to the lake, you go ahead."

Keith took precise instructions from Luise as to where they had seen the water spout, and Christine decided to go along too once she heard about the thunder clap and deafening noise from the dragonflies.

At that point, Brian came over to join them. "Just as I thought. The ventilation radiator has corroded, and the coolant is leaking out and getting into the ventilation system."

"Hasn't been sabotaged, I hope?" Jake asked, thinking that the two men they had met were capable of anything.

"Well, that's possible, of course—I hadn't thought of that. But the ventilation radiator is very difficult to access. You can't get at it. Boy, what a horrible smell. I'm hoping it's not the head gasket. It could be, with that smell. They call it the smell of death."

"Well, that sounds ominous," Tom remarked.

"Not another omen!" said Jake.

"Mein Gott! We've had so many omens today we could be in a Fontane novel," Luise joked. "Well, I'm sorry we can't stay on, but I do need some medical help, and we don't want to miss the last bus."

Luise, Jake, and Tom thanked the CNN team for their help and support and wished them all the best.

"We'll see you at the Glass Mountains—if not

before," said Patrick.

"Yes, if we can't get this coolant leak sorted, we might be joining you on the last bus!" Brian laughed.

"Keep in touch!" Helen called to them as they walked off up the road through the village, passing the church and Tudor-style buildings on the right and the museum on the left, where Lake Dagow and the bus terminus came into view.

They were silent for a while. Then Luise ventured, "So that's what the lake was trying to warn us about. Just like in Fontane's novel. The lake is communicating with us. That miniature eruption was a statement of some sort. And it sent out the swarming dragonflies as a warning."

Jake thought for a moment. "Well, I can tell you one thing. Those guys are from the U.S., and they have Californian accents. Not from the Midwest like me, that's for sure."

"All right. I would say we need to work out our next move once we get back to Berlin, and my shoulder has been seen to," Luise proposed.

Bus 836 arrived on schedule and took them to Gransee via Menz. Luise reminded them that the character in Fontane's novel *Quitt* who died on the Glass Mountains, was Lehnert Menz, so they asked the bus driver to stop for one minute just before the intersection with Berliner Strasse while they took selfies of themselves in front of the sixteenth century

Menz village church. As they were his only passengers, he was happy to do so. The bus then continued past fields of grazing cattle, sheep, and horses, rolling plowed pastures and forest—what Luise called the heartland of Brandenburg—to Gransee, where they caught the RE5 train, and they were back at Berlin Südkreuz station within an hour. From there, it was just a short bus ride on the 248 down Südwestkorso to Wiesbadener Strasse, where Jake and Tom were staying in the same university apartment complex, known as the IBZ, where they had stayed the last time they were in Berlin. As on the last occasion, this had been kindly arranged by Professor von Dietermann of the Technische Universität. Luise knew the IBZ well, as she had her yoga classes there.

"There is a medical center just round the corner, at Rüdersheimer Platz," she said.

Jake and Tom accompanied her there. Luckily they were able to give her an appointment almost immediately. She emerged from the surgery, greatly relieved.

"The doctor managed to push it back into the socket joint," she said. "He told me to keep it in a sling for the next five days and apply ice when I can, and he prescribed me pain relief."

"Time for a painful extraction? Or have you had enough painful extractions for today?" grinned Jake, as they walked back through the entrance into the courtyard of the IBZ complex. They gathered around what used to be Luise's favorite sculpture. It was called "inhibited freedom," but Jake and Tom agreed with Luise that it looked a lot more like a pair of molars that had just been extracted. "Or a pair of women's boots filled with concrete," Tom laughed, recalling what Luise had said about the sculpture the first time they had seen it back in April. It was now December, and the trees around it had shed almost all of their leaves, but there was a Christmas tree sitting in the middle of the courtyard, which gave some color to the grey surroundings.

"Thirty-nine steps up to our apartment," Jake joked, knowing that Luise had always counted the seventy steps up to her yoga classroom on the top floor.

"Just so long as it's not Alfred Hitchcock's *39 Steps*," commented Tom. "I'm not good at dealing with international spy rings."

"Well, Professor von Dietermann has got you a good place again," said Luise as she entered the apartment.

"Yes, a nice view over Wiesbadener Strasse," Jake agreed, taking her through the living room into the small study overlooking the busy street below. "Look, this is completely enclosed with windows, but they're all double glazed, and the door to the living room has thick glass too, so it gets nice and warm in the sunshine, but there's no heat loss. Triple glazing."

"Hardly any noise either," Tom commented. "Now, at long last, we've got a quiet place where we can just relax and discuss things—and not be overheard."

The trio sat down in the armchairs that surrounded the small table in the middle of the room.

"Well, first of all, let's just work through what those two creeps were saying," Tom suggested. "Who are they, and what do they represent? If they resort to violence like that, we have to take them seriously."

"There's obviously more to them than the CNN people reckon," said Jake. "They weren't just listening in on the interview. They seem to know all about me and where I live, and in many ways, my worst fears have been realized—they have all the data on my laptop. So they've got a lot of information about all of us and what we are doing."

"That's right. It's not quite as easy as the CNN team was saying," Tom remarked. "Patrick said we just needed to go to a place where they will never find us. But he admitted that was easier said than done. They would probably find us here pretty easily."

"Let's just think about what we experienced at the lake this afternoon," suggested Luise, adjusting the ice pack she was holding against her shoulder. "In Fontane's novel, the lake can warn you about outside events to protect you."

"In other words, it can give you advice?"

"Well, yes, Jake, in a manner of speaking."

"So how do we interpret the signs it was giving us?

"Let's start with the first one, Jake. The red water spout."

"You mean what I thought looked like a miniature Mt. Kilauea eruption — red vertical jetting?"

"Yes. In Fontane's novel, the lake is somehow connected to the South Pacific.

He writes about Lake Stechlin responding to eruptions in Hawaii that spread clouds of ash over the South Pacific."

"So if, as you say, Luise, in Fontane's novel, the lake is the main character and warns and advises people, what was it suggesting to us?" Tom asked. "Go to the South Pacific?"

"But where in the South Pacific?" Jake thought for a moment. "Not Mt. Kilauea, that's for sure. That wouldn't make any sense. Our biggest active volcano. From what I've read, it's far too dangerous."

"Well, Fontane writes about the parts of the Pacific that come within the Hawaiian volcanic ash zone," Luise elaborated.

"The volcanic ash zone is huge. Four-thousand miles, didn't you say, Jake?"

"You betcha! And didn't you work out that that includes some New Zealand territory, Tom?"

"Yes, Tokelau is only about two-thousand miles from Hawaii."

"But there is a huge part of the Pacific within that four-thousand-mile zone, isn't there, Jake?" Luise asked.

Jake looked at the map of the Pacific that he had brought up on his phone. "Yes, apart from the US territories and French Polynesia, there is Kiribati, the Solomon Islands, Vanuatu, Fiji, Samoa, Tonga —"

"So is the lake directing us towards a particular part of the Pacific?" asked Luise.

Tom looked at her triumphantly. "The Atafu omen!"

"You mean all those dragonflies?" Luise mused. "I thought they were pointing towards the wharf to warn us there was danger lurking there."

"Yes, Luise, but the Atafu omen is only associated with one place in the Pacific, and that's Tokelau, New Zealand territory."

"Well, New Zealand would be safer for us than here or Oklahoma," said Luise. "They know too much about us. But do you think you know somewhere in New Zealand where you think they could never find us, Tom?"

Tom thought for a while. "Yes, I can think of the ideal place. Snake Point!"

CHAPTER 5

"Snake Point?!" Jake and Luise cried out in unison.

"Sounds like another omen to me," said Jake. "Haven't we had enough of them?"

"No, not at all," Tom went on to explain. "Snake Point is a narrow peninsula, one of the nicest parts of the Marlborough Sounds. That's on the northern part of the South Island of New Zealand. It was named by the British explorer Captain Cook when he was based in Ship Cove there in the 1770s. From a distance, the peninsula looks like a snake entering the sea — that's why he called it Snake Point. My uncle owns a bach there — you would probably call it a cabin in America, Jake — a tiny holiday cottage with its own jetty. We used to go there every summer. It's like living on an island. No one would ever find us there."

"Sounds ideal. But wouldn't there be someone there this time of year?" asked Jake.

"Over Christmas, there is. But then people need to get back to work. I can contact Uncle Bill and see if we can get there after Christmas."

"All righty. The only problem there is how are we going to pay for our flights?"

"Well, Jake, how about we contact Judy Thorpe to see if there is any provision for this sort of thing in the United Nations STSM fund — remember the short-term scientific mission they set up for us? We will need to explain that we are due to go to Oklahoma in January for the launch of our manifesto on CNN, but we have decided New Zealand is the safest place at the moment for us to work on our manifesto undisturbed."

"Good idea, Luise. And Judy Thorpe is a New Zealander. She'll understand our situation. I'll call Dr. Lemaster at the University of Oklahoma, and perhaps we should all see Professor von Dietermann at the Technische Universität here as soon as possible to give him an update. But Tom, I think you should let Professor Aurisch at Auckland know, then contact Judy Thorpe. One New Zealander to another. Don't you think so, Luise?

"*Aber natürlich*! That's the best plan of action. Let's get to it straight away. If all goes according to plan, we could be in New Zealand by Boxing Day. That's what they called it when I was studying in St Andrews, anyway. What do they call it in Oklahoma,

Jake?"

"The day after Christmas. That's the big day for the post-Christmas sales in Oklahoma."

"In New Zealand it's the Boxing Day sales, so everything is open. A good day to arrive."

***

"Wow, Bill! What a spectacular view!"

"Yes, Jake, that's what they say — you can't beat Wellington on a fine day!"

Jake, Luise, and Tom were sitting with Tom's uncle Bill in the Kelburn Cable Car, on their way from Lambton Quay up to the Botanic Gardens. Bill had met them at Wellington Airport the previous afternoon and had put them up at his place by Trentham Memorial Park. They had gone for a brisk walk through Barton's Bush and along the Hutt River before having dinner, after which they went straight to sleep — "crashed," as Tom put it — after the long flight. Bill then suggested they spend a day exploring Wellington before catching the ferry to the Marlborough Sounds the following day to help them recover from their jet lag.

"I gather you're on a scientific mission in the Sounds. A day of relaxation seeing the sights of Wellington will allow you to concentrate," he had said.

They had boarded the Cable Car at Lambton Quay and had taken a lot of photos and videos as they headed through a series of tunnels, the second and third of which featured displays of moving colored lights. As they emerged from the third tunnel and passed what Bill said was the Salamanca stop for the university, a large vista started to open up before them. To their immediate right, they could see a sports field, and behind it a venerable old brick building with a number of modern buildings grouped around it. Bill said this was the main campus of Victoria University of Wellington, or Vic, as most people called it. On the far side of the sports field was a fountain, and beyond that could be seen a number of large city buildings extending over to the bush-covered slopes of Mount Victoria. A series of mountain peaks rose in the distance, which Bill said was the Tararua Ranges. To the left of Mount Victoria was a stunning view of Wellington Harbor, its sparkling blue colors reflecting the clear sunny sky.

"The entrance to the harbor is the other side of Mt. Victoria," explained Bill. "That's the way the ferry will take you tomorrow, then across the Cook Strait through the Marlborough Sounds to Picton. From there, you'll take another boat to Snake Point on Queen Charlotte Channel. We call our place Innisfree."

"Innisfree? Isn't that a poem by Yeats?" Luise asked.

"Yes, my aunt named it that after the poem. 'I will arise and go now, and go to Innisfree, and a small cabin build there.'"

"I remember that poem up on the wall in the bach. Isn't there something about peace?" asked Tom.

"Yes, that's right. 'And I shall have some peace there, for peace comes dropping slow.'"

"Well, I hope that's right because that's what we're needing, in more ways than one," Jake commented.

At that moment, the cable car reached its final stop, Kelburn, and Bill took them over to see the original cable car in the Cable Car Museum.

"This used to be packed full of students on their way to the university in my day," Bill explained. "We used to sit on the outside seats and do our last-minute swotting for our tests coming up. These days most students take the bus, number 22, which runs straight from the train station."

From there, they walked to the entrance to the Botanic Gardens.

"What's that tree over there with all the lovely big red flowers?" asked Luise. "I've never seen anything like it before."

"That's a pohutukawa—they call it the New Zealand Christmas Tree," Bill replied. "This time of the year, they are always covered with red blossoms. My favorite tree. That's why I brought you here. They've adopted the pohutukawa blossom as the symbol of the Botanic Gardens—you'll see it imprinted in the concrete along the main pathway. Follow the pohutukawa, and you won't get lost."

Just past the Australian garden, they found a huge grove of magnificent pohutukawa in full blossom, and that was the occasion for selfies and group shots "for the whanau back home," as Jake put it, borrowing Tom's phrase. "The folks back home will really love this. They've never been further south than Houston, Texas, and they didn't like it there at all."

They then passed a large kauri, said to have been gifted by Sir George Grey, New Zealand's governor, from 1845.

"He would have brought it down from Auckland. Auckland is full of them," Tom pointed out. "But a lot of the walking tracks in the Auckland ranges have been closed because the kauri have been affected by some sort of dieback disease. This is the healthiest one I've seen for a long time."

More selfies were taken there and from the "treehouse," an elevated building with great views of the surrounding trees, and all three of them wanted their photos taken sitting in Basil's seat, a park bench flanked by a sculptured bush resembling a sleeping cat.

"It's dedicated to Basil, the cat. He used to live around the tree house and befriended everyone that walked along this track," Bill told them.

He then suggested they return to the cable car end of the track so they could walk down past the university, as there was something he wanted to show them on the way down to Parliament Grounds, which was their next stop. They walked down Rawhiti Terrace and into the Hub, an internal courtyard that linked all the main university buildings.

"Although it's a lovely calm day today, the wind, which they call the Wellington Whisper, can get quite blustery, and this is a nice way to shelter from the weather," Bill smiled.

"A bit like the Lichthof at the Technische Universität in Berlin," remarked Luise.

"Yes, and like the one at the University in Zürich," added Tom. "A nice friendly atmosphere at all times of the year."

"I remember the one in Zürich well," said Bill. "I used to think the same — until the friendly atmosphere suddenly collapsed on me when the ceiling came down during an Old High German lecture!"

They all listened intently as Bill told them about the hunks of plaster that had come crashing down around him and were intrigued to hear that the lecturer kept going as if nothing had happened.

Bill then took the trio to the fifth floor in the lift.

"Did you like Zürich, then, Tom?" asked Bill.

"Yes, it was everything you said it would be. But I can see how depressing that fog can get in the winter."

"You know, I used to go to the opera there practically every second night to get a bit of color into my life. Quite different here. The Wellington whisper doesn't give fog a chance!"

They were all laughing as the lift doors opened, and Bill took them from there to the front of the building. Jake was the first to reach the windows overlooking the harbor. "Wow! What a view!" They all gathered around to have a look.

"Yes, Wellington's best kept secret," Bill grinned. They had a clear view of the wide expanse of the harbor from Mt. Victoria and Oriental Bay on their right all the way over to the motorway on the left. "And if you follow the line of the motorway, you can see the Hutt Valley in the middle distance."

"Can we see the park where we went for a walk with you after we arrived yesterday from here?" asked Jake.

"You mean Trentham Memorial Park? See where the hill comes down from the right? That's the Taita Gorge that divides the upper and lower valleys. Look a bit further up there, and you'll see a hill on the left with a big patch of native bush. That's on the other side of the river from Bartons Bush, where I took you for that walk yesterday."

"And that's a park of some sort over there just below us, with the fountain?" asked Jake.

"Yes, that's Kelburn Park."

"Well, the fountain is vertical jetting just like Kilauea," Jake commented.

"And what section of the library is this?" Luise asked.

"Turn around and have a look," said Bill.

Luise was delighted to find her favorite books behind her. "Fontane! And *Quitt* on the top shelf — with *Lake Stechlin* next to it!"

"Yes! I guess you could say Fontane has the best view of Wellington," said Bill.

They all chuckled at that idea.

"Well, the signs are telling us we're in the right place," said Tom.

Bill pointed out the large inter-island ferry, which was plying its way across the harbor.

"That's the *Kaitaki*," he said, pointing to a large white ship glistening in the sun in the middle of the harbor, with an orange strip above its upper deck. "The interislander. This time tomorrow, you'll be on board. It gets you to Picton in the Marlborough Sounds in just over three hours. But that's tomorrow. What we're going to do now before I drive you back home is have a quick look at Parliament Grounds."

From the University Library, they walked down Salamanca Road and The Terrace to Parliament Buildings, dominated at that point by the "Beehive," a distinctive ten-floor circular building rising in steps that, Bill explained, housed the prime minister, cabinet minsters, and their advisors. They walked around the front of the Beehive to the statue of Richard John Seddon. Seddon was New Zealand's longest-serving prime minister, Tom explained, from 1893 to 1906. This was a crucial time in New Zealand's history, as it was during his time as prime minister that New Zealand decided not to join the Australian Commonwealth but to "go it alone," as he put it, establishing its own South Pacific dominion.

"So that's how Tokelau became part of New Zealand then, Tom?" asked Luise.

"Yes, Seddon went on a tour of the Pacific Islands in 1900, pointing out to island leaders the advantages of becoming part of a New Zealand South Pacific dominion. As a result, New Zealand took over the administration of many Pacific islands — the Cook Islands in 1900, Niue the following year, and Tokelau later on. Tokelau had been a British protectorate since 1889. That way, New Zealand could form its own South Pacific dominion and didn't need to be part of Australia."

Remembering the connection with Lake Stechlin, Jake, Tom, and Luise took numerous selfies with the statue of Seddon and the Beehive and Parliament Buildings behind them and asked Bill to take group photos as well. Bill then took them through the parliamentary gardens, where they admired the huge pohutukawa trees covered with red blossoms. Bill took a number of group photos of them standing at a point where the pohutukawa trees had created a red carpet of blossoms on the roadway where it wound down to the entrance to the parliament buildings. Luise then walked up to admire the rose gardens in front of the General Assembly Library and was taken by the loud buzzing of the bees. As she looked around, she noticed some dragonflies among them.

"Dragonflies! Now that fits in nicely with our omens and prefigurations. We really could be in a Fontane novel!"

"Is Lake Stechlin still keeping an eye on us? Giving us subtle warnings?" Tom ventured.

"Hmm. I wonder if it was the right decision to go to Snake Point," Jake observed.

"Well, you'll soon find out," said Bill. "This time tomorrow, you'll be there."

CHAPTER 6

"This is the most dangerous part of the Cook Strait crossing—the entrance to Tory Channel. A lot of boats have gone down here!" As Tom pointed to the treacherous looking rocks they were passing, Jake and Luise leaned over the starboard side of the ship to get a better view. "But it does get calmer from now on. We've left Cook Strait behind us, and we are now in the Marlborough Sounds."

"It looks like we're completely out of the fog now, Tom," said Luise.

"Yes, there's often fog on Cook Strait, even in the most beautiful weather, and

the ferry has to use its fog horn."

"So is this the South Island now, then?" asked Jake.

"Yes, this is the South Island—larger in size, but smaller in population than the North Island. But some people would say it's more scenic."

"It sure looks pretty from here," commented Jake. "Does anyone live around here?"

"Not so many around Tory Channel, though there is some oyster farming. It's mainly holiday houses here, what we call baches, in the sheltered bays — here are some coming up now."

As the ship proceeded, the channel opened up to a number of bays with sheltered beaches, each with a sprinkling of houses nestled in small valleys of wild pine and regenerating bush, with gullies of native fern. A number of small fishing boats were out trying their luck a short distance from the beach.

Luise was ecstatic. "Wunderbar! Is Snake Point anything like this?"

"Well, we'll be seeing it soon. It comes into sight as soon as we pass Dieffenbach Point on the left, and that's it coming up now."

"Dieffenbach? Sounds like a German name to me."

"Yes, he was, Luise. He was a medical graduate from Giessen, best known here as an early German explorer."

Luise made sure she took a selfie of herself with Dieffenbach Point in the background. "My first selfie without a sling! I'm sure Dr. Dieffenbach would approve!"

As the ship moved out into Queen Charlotte Sound, it started to turn left, and a number of peninsulas came into view on the other side. One was particularly prominent, a tall forest-covered hill with a long point projecting into the sea. The headland was characterized by a prominent ridge, extending all the way from the top of the hill down to the rocks that surrounded the point.

Tom turned to the others and pointed excitedly across to the other side of the channel. "That's Snake Point!"

Luise and Jake took out their phones to capture the view.

"I can see why Captain Cook called it Snake Point," Luise commented. "It does look like a snake."

"Or a crocodile with its head half-submerged," said Jake. "The big windows on that house up on the ridge look like its eyes, the rocks are its teeth, and the red bit at the end is its tongue."

"What is the red bit at the end?" asked Luise.

"That's a pohutukawa," Tom explained. "There are lots of them in blossom around here. Just like the ones in Wellington."

"Snake Point looks like a crocodile about to snap," Jake observed.

"Or a snake about to bite," Luise laughed. "Reminds me of those two horrible men at Lake Stechlin. Hope it's not an omen. Where is your place, Tom? Innisfree?"

"It's a bit further along, just down from the

house with the eyes. You can see our green boathouse just past the rocks about halfway along the peninsula. And then, just a bit further along, you can see our jetty. That's where we'll be dropped off later this afternoon. We'll be catching the local ferry from Picton."

"So the interislander berths in Picton?" Jake asked.

"Yes. Picton's about half an hour from here, at the end of Queen Charlotte Sound."

Luise and Jake took more videos as they watched Snake Point slowly disappear into the distance.

"It looks like Snake Point is at the entrance to something else behind it," commented Jake.

"Yes, that's the Bay of Many Coves," said Tom. "You'll find out why it's called that when we go back there this afternoon. The boat always goes in there before it gets to Snake Point."

Intrigued and taken by the beauty of the landscape, Jake and Luise took more and more photos and videos as the ship passed bays, coves, and islands. They passed a salmon farm with a large floating shed completely covered with seagulls. Jake commented that they looked like decorative stones on the roof. They took photos of what they called five more "little snake points," small peninsulas disappearing into the sea. On the left, signs of civilization started to appear in the form of a small seaside settlement which Tom said was Waikawa Bay, and then in front of them, they could see the wharves of Picton Harbor. Once it pulled up alongside the logging wharf, the ferry reversed into the interislander terminal at Picton, and from there, it was only a short walk across the foreshore reserve to the wharves, where the trio boarded the small local ferry that would take them to Snake Point.

"This ferry is very popular with the tourists because it goes right down the channel to Ship's Cove, which is the start of the Queen Charlotte Track," said Tom. "But it's also the lifeline for the people that live in the Marlborough Sounds. It drops people off and collects them from their jetties and also delivers provisions. You can always tell the tourists from where they sit. They like to sit on the seats at the back of the boat — they don't realize how windy and wet it gets there. If you want to sit outside, you have to sit behind the cabin, so you're sheltered from the wind."

Luise and Jake took Tom's advice and sat with him behind the upstairs cabin, where they had a good view of the harbor and bays they were passing. Once they were out of the harbor, the boat picked up speed. Sure enough, it was not long before the passengers sitting at the back first put up their hoodies, then decided they had had enough of the strong breeze and being splashed by the wake, and packed up their food and drink and went inside. The view was now totally unobstructed. After Picton receded into the distance and Waikawa Bay appeared to the right, the boat turned north into Ruakaka Bay, where they passed a number of small houses nestled in the bush and stopped at a jetty to drop off some passengers.

"Bay of Many Coves will be the next stop, and then Snake Point," said Tom. "But you can see Snake Point at the entrance to the Bay of Many Coves. Just around the next corner."

The boat passed a large king salmon farm as it left Ruakaka Bay, swung east around the next promontory, then headed north as it entered the Bay of Many Coves, and they could immediately appreciate what an appropriate name that was. However, Tom focussed their attention on Snake Point.

"There it is! That's Snake Point right in front of us. Innisfree is on the other side. Our home for the next few days."

Jake and Luise took shots of the pohutukawa in full bloom at the point, which Luise referred to as the snake's tongue. As the boat headed into the Bay of Many Coves, they focussed on the large house on the ridge with its huge glass windows, which Jake called the snake's eyes. The boat dropped off some provisions at the resort, then swung back towards the entrance to the Bay of Many Coves, passing the outcrop of rocks at the end of the point, which Jake reminded them was the snake's teeth. "Or the crocodile's teeth, depending on what you think you're looking at."

The boat then proceeded around the point and

up the Sound, and they noticed a number of houses on the ridge.

"These houses have a really good view of the Bay of Many Coves and the channel, but they're exposed to a lot of wind. Our place is on the hillside, sheltered from the northwesterlies," said Tom.

They passed a pine forest punctuated by valleys with native bush, many of them with jetties servicing holiday homes. They also noticed a number of slips, which Tom said were very common in areas where steep cliffs met the sea. Just along from one slip was a clearing with a large pohutukawa on the seashore. On the ridge above was the house with the big windows. Then a large green boathouse came into view, with a nicely mown lawn next to it and behind it native bush extending right up to the ridge.

"That's our boathouse," said Tom. "And further along the beach, you can see our jetty."

As the boat started to approach the jetty, they could see a natural valley of the native bush up to the ridge. About a third of the way up the hill, above the boathouse, were two small buildings, one green, partly obscured by trees, and one light brown.

"That's our bach and our cabin," said Tom. "Welcome to Innisfree!"

"What a lovely spot," Luise commented. "Perfect for writing our manifesto!"

They all disembarked from the back of the local

ferry, as it was high tide, and waved to the skipper and passengers as it departed.

"Is that a kiwi?" Luise asked, pointing to a brown hen-like wingless bird strutting down the path towards them.

"No, that's a weka, coming down to welcome us," Tom explained. "They're flightless and brown, just like a kiwi. Very friendly birds. They always look after us here."

"Ah, *Gast der Natur*, as we say in German. We're nature's guests. And what are the loud insects? All that buzzing? Are they welcoming us here too?"

"Yes, they are the cicadas. They tend to be pretty noisy this time of the year. Cicadas and dragonflies."

"Dragonflies!" Jake laughed. "I thought we left them behind in Wellington! Well, I hope they're not too much of a Lake Stechlin omen."

Tom told them about the path up to the bach. "It's a zig-zag path with steps. Each zig has steps in it as it meets each zag. There are thirty-nine steps altogether, two hundred-and-two with the zig-zags, but the zigs and zags are quite long, and the pedometer on my phone showed three-hundred-and-twenty-eight. So take your pick!"

"Thirty-nine steps? We're back in the Alfred Hitchcock movie!" Jake laughed.

"So it's further than the steps up to the IBZ in Berlin then?" Luise asked.

"A lot further. So take as much as you can with you."

Each of them put on their backpacks and carried two boxes of provisions up the zig-zag path to the bach, Tom leading the way. He unlocked the bach and the neighboring cabin.

Tom turned to the others. "This is one of the most isolated places in the world. No one will find us here. Now, theoretically, we could have a building each. One in the boathouse, one in the bach, and one in the cabin. But it would make more sense for us all to stick together up here, two in the bach and one in the cabin, because this is where the kitchen and the toilet are, and there's plenty of room."

They eventually decided that Tom and Jake would share the bach, and Luise would sleep in the cabin.

"The cabin has the best view of the bay," said Luise. "I just love the sea views from here. But it also means I can keep an eye out for any passing vessels — and anyone landing at the jetty. No one will be able to land here without me seeing."

"In that case, you'll be on sentry duty, and we'll have our meetings in the cabin so we can keep an eye on the bay and the jetty. The cabin will be the perfect spot for sorting out our manifesto," Tom remarked and took them into the bach. "Now, here are the solar power points for charging any devices, and it's just a matter of connecting up the fridge. How about you two get everything set up here, and I'll go down and check out the boatshed and the beach. Then we can get stuck into the manifesto tomorrow morning."

Jake and Luise were happy to get everything set up at the bach and the cabin, so Tom set off down the zig-zag to the jetty and boatshed. As he came out of the bush into the clearing at the bottom of the hill, he noticed something unusual. It looked like a big black and white dog standing by the jetty. As he came closer, he realized it was a large goat eating the newly mown grass, with a smaller grey-colored goat grazing next to him. On seeing the goat's horns, Tom thought this pair was most likely to be a billy-goat and a nanny-goat, and he approached them carefully. However, as soon as they caught sight of Tom, they bolted off to the right, tearing past the back of the boatshed and along the beach. Tom tried following them, but they were too fast for him and disappeared around the bend, so he gave up, thinking it was more important at this stage to check the boatshed.

He unlocked the boatshed, then opened up the roller door and took out a chair so he could sit above the boat ramp and get a good view of his surroundings. On the left, he could see the jetty at the end of the grassy clearing, and on the hill above it a belt of tall pines leading down to a promontory, beyond which was Queen Charlotte Sound, with a number of yachts, fishing boats, and motor boats making their way to and from Picton. Opposite was Arapawa Island with its numerous inlets, dotted with pines, and to the right was the entrance to Tory Channel, where Tom could see the Wellington Ferry making its way past Dieffenbach Point. To his immediate right was the stony beach the goats had disappeared along, with a number of fallen pines. Just beyond the beach, he could see the pohutukawa they had seen from the local ferry that had dropped them off just two hours earlier. Tom decided to head in that direction, not just to see if he could find the goats but also to check out the small bach he remembered used to be behind the pohutukawa tree. As far as he knew, no one had stayed in that bach for years. *But who knows?* he thought. If there was someone there, he had a neighborly duty to drop in and say hello.

He set out towards the point, clambering over the fallen pine trees, some of which covered the entire beach. He managed to climb over or squeeze under five of the tree trunks, and luckily the sixth was split in two in the middle, so it was just a matter of pushing himself through the middle, and then the pohutukawa was just in front of him. He walked around to the right of the pohutukawa into the trees behind. As he entered the dense bush behind the pohutukawa, the sound of the cicadas and dragonflies, which had been a pleasant humming in the background up until then, suddenly escalated into a deafening high-pitched buzzing sound.

Something hit him from behind. He turned around and found hundreds of dragonflies swarming behind him, flying around in aimless circles and hitting whatever was in their way. Before he could even start thinking about whether this might be another Lake Stechlin omen, he suddenly became aware, through the trees of the hidden bach he was looking for, of a rectangular building painted in a shade of dark green that was almost impossible to make out through the trees. As he approached the building, he heard an almighty crash.

CHAPTER 7

Tom ran around the back of the building to see what had happened. There he found the two goats. The large black and white one had obviously taken fright and crashed into the back of the bach, catching its horns in some vines growing in and around the back of the building, and was stuck. When the smaller grey goat spied Tom, it rushed off into the undergrowth. Tom got out his pocket knife and cut the vines back to free the black and white goat. For a moment, it looked intently at Tom, and Tom thought it was about to charge him, but then it turned tail, and with a little bleat that sounded as if it was thanking Tom, bolted off into the undergrowth.

Tom then moved forward to look at the bach. It turned out to consist of two small adjoining buildings, both made of corrugated iron and painted dark green, capped with an iron roof. Although he had not seen anyone staying here for some years, there were signs that the back door had been opened recently. *It must be possible to stay here without being seen from our place,* he thought. That was something he must tell the others.

He then pushed past the pohutukawa and made his way back along the beach, past the six fallen pine trees to the boathouse, and then back up the zig-zag to the bach. Luise and Jake greeted him with great excitement.

"Our CNN interview has been on already! We've been watching it on our phones. And they even talk about the launch of our manifesto on the Glass Mountains!"

Tom watched the clip on Jake's phone. "Wow! They've really done us proud! And all those drone shots. Fantastic! Getting Fontane's message through. 'If mankind is to survive, we must get beyond the mentality of revenge.' And they obviously liked your bit about resolving international rivalry, Luise."

"I bet those two dumbheads at Lake Stechlin didn't like it, though," said Jake. "They'll be after us."

"And we have to be on the lookout for people all the time," said Tom. He told them about what he had seen, which showed that it must be possible for people to arrive at the neighboring bach without being noticed. He said that although the goats were a bit of a nuisance, he ended up feeling quite grateful to them, as otherwise, he would not have noticed the back door had been opened so recently.

This sobering thought meant they had quite a muted dinner. By the time they finished, the sun had disappeared from the top of the hills on the other side of the channel, and as it was getting dark, Tom thought of something that would cheer them up—he suggested they go down to the jetty. They took their torches and navigated their way down the zig-zags, dodging cicadas and dragonflies doing their last circuits of the day, buzzing around aimlessly in every direction. They walked onto the jetty and looked out over the bay. On the other side of the channel, a small yacht could be seen heading out to sea with a bright red port light. In the far distance, a dim light could be seen, probably the interior light of a house in one of the inlets. Apart from the sound of low-flying birds fluttering past, some of them in formation, looking for fish, all that could be heard was the gentle lapping of the water against the shore. It was so quiet the wekas were able to call to each other across the bay. Looking over to the right, they could see the Wellington Ferry come into view as it started to head across to enter Tory Channel.

"The wake from the ferry takes twenty minutes to get here. Then the lapping of the water turns to a swishing sound for a couple of minutes. I've got something I want to show you, and it's best to see it when it's completely calm, so let's do it now," said Tom, leaning over the side of the jetty and dipping a stick into the water. "Look!"

As he moved the stick around in the water, little sparklets darted out in all directions. It was as if he were generating electricity in the water.

"What causes that, Tom? Can I have a go?" asked Jake.

"It's called luminescence," Tom replied. "It only happens in unpolluted waters."

Luise ran off to find some more sticks, and it was not long before all three of them were swishing their sticks backwards and forwards in the water, watching the sparks leap up and down, some of them meeting each other in mid-air.

They were all shrieking with delight when suddenly, out of nowhere, they heard a voice behind them. Startled, they spun around to find that someone had crept up on them in a kayak.

"Geez, where did you come from!" Tom yelled.

"Hi! Sorry to give you a fright! I'm Robert Shannon from along the bay. I saw your torches and thought I'd come over and say hello. I'm down here for a week, staying with my mum. Our bach is just down there on the other side of the pohutukawa."

"Oh yes, I remember your family," said Tom. "We went out fishing with your dad a couple of years ago and caught lots of gurnard. The other side of the pohutukawa, eh? I just had a look at the bach down there and was surprised to see it's still being used. I haven't seen anyone there for years."

"Every now and then, there's someone there, but they tend to come and go at times you wouldn't expect them, and they don't stay long," Robert explained.

"I see. Well, how about some introductions. I'm Tom Furlonger. These are my friends, Luise Breitenbach and Jake Nickel. Luise's from Berlin in Germany, and Jake's from Oklahoma in the United States."

There were handshakes all around.

"So you're both on holiday here in New Zealand?" Robert asked.

"Well, sort of," Jake responded. "We're working together on an international research project, and Tom thought this would be the ideal place to get everything sorted out. Nice and quiet, and no noisy neighbors."

"Haha!" Robert laughed. "Well, the wekas can be a bit noisy sometimes when they try to wake up their friends across the bay with their screeching. And the goats get a bit carried away sometimes. But as far as humans are concerned, there's hardly anyone around at the moment. There's no one next door in the bach behind the pohutukawa, so we're your closest neighbors. If you ever need help with anything, just let us know. We're ten minutes along the beach or five minutes by kayak, and I know there are kayaks in your boatshed."

They thanked Robert as he moved off into the darkness.

"Oh, by the way," Robert added. "If you're from Berlin, you've probably never seen glowworms. There are some just along here behind the boathouse."

Robert paddled over to the bank behind the boathouse and pointed to a deep recess in the bank. Luise moved over to have a look, followed by the others. Sure enough, in the sheltered area under the top part of the overlapping bank, there were a number of glowworms, sending out their pulsating blue light into the surrounding darkness.

Luise was overjoyed. "*Glühwürme*! Glowworms! *Mein Gott*! You're quite right. I've never seen anything like it. First luminescence, and now this! This is an amazing place! *Wunderbar!*"

At that, Robert waved a cheery goodbye, paddled off around the boathouse, and disappeared into the darkness.

"Well, it's good to know we've got nice neighbors," commented Jake as they walked back up to the bach. "But it does show you we have to be on our guard. Particularly if there might be someone staying in the bach behind the pohutukawa. Motorboats and ferries make a lot of noise. But people can arrive by kayak or rowboat, and we wouldn't even know they're here."

***

"Okay, time to call a meeting of the 'Glass Mountains Mission' to discuss our manifesto," said Tom as they gathered together in the cabin the following morning after breakfast. They sat around a small table facing the window, so they could keep an eye on the jetty and "be inspired by the view," as Luise put it. It was Hans-Ulrich Menz in the Fontane Archives in Potsdam who first called the trio the "Glass Mountains Mission," and Judy Thorpe, Special Envoy for Conflict Resolution at the United Nations, adopted the term when she last met with them. They rather liked it.

"How about we call this the 'Glass Mountains Manifesto'?" suggested Jake.

"Good idea," said Luise. "But first of all, we would need to explain Fontane's message and the connection with the Glass Mountains. How he set much of his anti-war novel *Quitt* in a Mennonite mission station in the Indian Territory, and how the climax takes place in the mountains close by—the Glass Mountains. And how Fontane got one of his Mennonite contacts there to hide his message for the future in a little box buried in a position that could not be identified till the summer solstice of 2019 when the reflected sun's rays converged on that spot. The year of the two-hundredth anniversary of his birth. He obviously thought no one was listening in 1890 when he wrote it but hoped someone might be a hundred-and-twenty years later."

"An introduction. I like that," said Tom. "You write that bit then. Now for the cryptic message itself. Obadja: 24. We managed to work out that Fontane was referring to Obadja's sermon in Chapter 24 of his novel *Quitt* — the last three pages of Chapter 24. Here Obadja is exploring alternatives to war. He says we must get beyond the idea of revenge. So much war and conflict have arisen simply because people want to get their revenge on others. He quotes the Bible twice as saying that we must stop thinking about revenge and leave it all to God. Just like the end of *The Revenant*, when Hugh Glass remembers what Hikuc had said about revenge and sends Fitzgerald downstream to the Arikara with the words, 'Revenge is in God's hands…not mine.'"

"Exactly!" said Jake. "Romans chapter 12, verse 19. 'Vengeance is mine; I will repay, saith the Lord.' In other words, take revenge out of your thinking. It's not worth it. Revenge will only turn out to be worse in the long run. Think of the sports field. If a player punches you and you punch him back, you both get sent off. It's not worth it. And is there revenge in nature? I don't think so. Now, what about the model Fontane puts forward? Luise, I remember you said that in his novel, he invents a multi-lingual, multi-racial, multi-religious community as a model which he hopes Europe and the world will follow? As I understand it, the community Obadja runs is much more than a mission station."

"Yes, Jake, we need to emphasize that Obadja's message is aimed at everyone in his community, not just the Mennonites. Lots of people of other faiths, beliefs, and ethnicities are listening intently — indigenous Americans, Roman Catholics, Lutherans, and even L'Hermite, the avowed atheist."

"Absolutely," Tom agreed. "Professor Aurisch made it clear that all beliefs and ethnicities are welcome in Obadja's community. That is Fontane's ideal of a civilized state, a tolerant and considerate entity governed by common sense, instead of being besotted with the idea of military revenge, which is how Fontane saw Germany in the late nineteenth century."

"We also need to stress Fontane's concern about the escalation of the arms race," Jake suggested.

"*Richtig*! Absolutely right," Luise agreed. "That's so important. International rivalry got so bad towards the end of the nineteenth century it was clear that war could break out at any time, and Fontane knew the consequences would be disastrous. Get rid of that revenge mentality. Why always resort to war? There must be some other way to settle differences."

"Yes, but we also need to remember what Dr. Lemaster said," Jake reminded the others. "It's not just an anti-war message. It goes much deeper than that. The idea of overcoming the mentality of revenge applies to all levels of our interaction, from our families to our workplace. Disputes escalate into conflicts."

"That's what Professor Aurisch said too," Tom agreed. "For him, Fontane is saying we need to completely change the way we associate with people — our families, friends, and workmates."

"I thought Judy Thorpe summarized it well," Luise reflected. "As she saw it, Fontane's message for the future is essentially that we have to rise above the mentality of revenge in our everyday life to stop disputes from escalating. As far as escalation to war is concerned, she suggested that perhaps something could be done to institute pre-conflict resolution in high-risk zones."

"Well, I think we've got more than enough material there," said Tom. "How about we write it all down now? This is our chance to sort out a really good manifesto while we're here by ourselves, with no one to interfere or disturb us."

All three sat down at their laptops and worked for a good two hours on their various sections of the manifesto, comparing notes as they went, and they were really pleased with the manifesto that started to emerge. In fact, they were so thoroughly engrossed in their project they initially did not notice that a kayak had arrived at their jetty.

"*Mein Gott*! *Wir haben Besuch*!" Luise yelped. "We've got a visitor! Look! Someone's down at the jetty!"

CHAPTER 8

Jake jumped up and took the binoculars from the shelf. "It's two visitors, actually. One of them might be Robert from last night. Let's go down and see."

At that, they all saved their work, put their laptops away, and ran down the zig-zag track to the jetty. Tom managed to get there first, but Jake and Luise were not far behind him.

He was right. It was Robert Shannon and a female passenger. By the time they arrived, Robert had paddled the kayak up to the beach just next to the jetty and was pulling it onto the stones so his passenger could get out.

"Hi, Tom. This is my mum!"

"Hi, Tom. I'm Ray. I remember you from years back."

"Ah yes, Ray. And your husband's Henry, right?"

"Yes, that's right. I'm one of Henry's many wives," she joked, winking at the others. To general laughter, they all shook hands as Tom introduced Ray to Luise and Jake.

"Well, we're here because of something potentially serious, actually," said Ray once the introductions and general merriment had died down. "Early this morning, a group of three men arrived at the bach by the pohutukawa, between your place and ours. They didn't leave their dinghy moored to the buoy, as you might normally expect, but hauled it right up to the beach and then carried it through the trees to the old bach. So if you hadn't seen them arrive, you wouldn't know they were there."

"I see. So there is someone there now. We were half expecting that after what Robert told us last night, and I noticed when I checked out the bach yesterday that the back door had been opened quite recently. We didn't see anyone arriving, though."

"Well, they seemed to be behaving suspiciously. Our property adjoins theirs, and we can see quite a lot from up in the trees. So I sent Robert up to have a look."

"And what did you see, Robert?"

"That's what worries us. They were carrying guns."

"Guns? Do you think they are off hunting goats? Some people do hunt goats up on the ridge here."

"Well, yes, that's true, Tom," Robert replied. "They were carrying rifles. But they seemed to have a whole case of ammunition with them. I've never seen anything like that before. I reckon they are up to no good."

"Where I come from, they would probably have more guns in the ammunition case," Jake ventured. "But the laws are different here."

"Yes, here you can only have guns for rifle range practice and hunting, and you have to have a license," said Robert.

"That's the same in Germany," Luise remarked.

They all stood quietly for a while.

Then Robert broke the silence. "Well, my plan is that I'll keep an eye on them. I can get quite close to their bach on our property, and the trees are so dense they would never see me. I'll see what they're up to. How about we exchange cell phone numbers so I can send you a message or call you if necessary? Apart from that, I can come down here to give you regular updates. I'll bring the kayak down. I always row down here anyway."

"Right-oh, that's a good idea. Thanks! Let's all stay in touch," Tom proposed, and they all exchanged cell phone numbers, assuring Ray in particular that if she was there by herself and needed any assistance, they would be there straight away, via the beach at low tide, or by boat, or along the ridge track if the sea was too rough.

"Yes, that ridge track is quite a climb, but it can be a real lifesaver in an emergency," commented Ray.

"I haven't taken them up there yet," said Tom.

"Is it much further up the hill from the bach, Tom?" Jake asked.

"Well, according to the health app on my phone, it's three-hundred-and-eighty steps from here to the bach and another fourteen-hundred up to the ridge."

"And it's not zig-zag, it's straight up!" added Ray, telling the others that she used to walk along the ridge a lot when she came there on her school holidays. "And I always used to leave a note in the message bottle up there. That was our main means of communication in those days. Neighbors from both sides of the ridge would leave messages — before we got cell phones!"

At that, she and Robert donned their lifejackets and got back into the kayak, and Tom helped push it into the water. Robert rowed out beyond the jetty and then headed towards the point. Both turned and waved before they disappeared behind the boatshed.

Luise decided it was now time for lunch, so they all headed back up to the bach, where Jake heated up some baked beans and sausages, and Tom made the toast while Luise stewed some apples. "Not quite Apfelstrudel, but getting close," she joked.

After lunch, they sat on the verandah of the

cabin, looking out over the bay. Jake kept his binoculars trained on anything that looked suspicious, but any yacht or barge or water taxi he focussed on simply continued on its journey to or from Picton. There was great excitement at one point when a cruise ship came past, flying a French flag. It seemed like a multi-story building gliding past, as high as the ridge above them. Tom explained that quite a number of tourist ships used Queen Charlotte Sound, as it was regarded as safer than Tory Channel, which was reserved for the ferries.

They were all starting to relax and enjoy the rippling water and the bird life around the bay when suddenly they heard two loud explosions from above them.

"Gunshots!" shouted Jake, and jumped up. "There's another one! Coming from this direction!" He pointed towards the top of the hill behind them.

"Are you sure?" asked Luise.

"I know a gunshot when I hear one!" Jake replied.

"Up on the ridge! Right-oh, let's climb up there and have a look. I'll text Robert and Ray, so they know what's going on," said Tom. "Make sure you've got shoes with good tread on them. It's really steep. And fourteen hundred steps, remember!"

"Aren't we putting our lives at risk, though?" Luise cautioned. "Might be something to do with those men at Lake Stechlin."

"The forest is so dense up there there's no problem in keeping ourselves concealed and out of danger," Tom reassured her. "We do need to know what's going on."

Luise decided her soles were all right, but Jake changed into his boots, and the three of them took off. Initially, there was a path, but that soon turned into a precipitous upward slope.

"Luckily, there are lots of manuka trees all the way up, so you can grab them for traction." Tom showed them how they could tell a manuka by its tiny leaves. "Manuka trees can be so useful. And not just for manuka honey. Just grab a manuka branch and swing yourself up. You can't trust any of the other trees, though. And anything that looks dead will just break. We don't want any more dislocated shoulders. From here, we're following the hill practically straight up. Every now and then, there's a piece of blue wire on a tree that tells you you're going the right way. My cousin put it up for his crystal radio set years ago. Now it's a welcome reminder that we're on the right track."

Jake and Luise took Tom's advice and followed him up the hill, grabbing hold of manuka branches and swinging their way up the slope. Luise tried not to use her left arm too much, seeing her left shoulder was still healing, and Jake followed close behind her, just in case there were any problems. The three of them enjoyed the rhythmical movement, though.

"I reckon we should patent this exercise," Jake laughed. "The manuka shuffle!"

Eventually, they emerged from the manuka and found themselves facing a group of large pine trees.

"We're practically on the ridge now," said Tom. "These pine trees are the edge of the pine plantation that extends right up to the summit. The ridge track takes you to the summit in one direction and the point in the other."

"So we're almost there?" gasped Jake. "Just as well! This is as bad as trying to wrestle the American University Eagles!"

They scrambled through the pines and past the gorse into a clearing. To their left was a wide path covered with brown pine needles, bordered on both sides by tall pine trees, which made its way downhill through a pine forest. To their right, the path had almost completely been overgrown with gorse and a variety of tussock grass, which Tom said was called toetoe.

Tom suggested they go and look at the view from further towards the point till they got their breath back. They walked down the path through the pine trees until they came to a clearing. Further down the slope in front of them was the house they had seen from the ferry, with its huge windows.

"Ah — so this is the house I called the crocodile's eyes," said Jake. "The eyes of Snake Point! It doesn't seem to have any conventional outside walls at all. All completely glass. Tinted glass. Amazing."

"A bit like the IBZ in Berlin, then," said Luise. "It must be double or even triple-glazed. But you can see why they built it that way. What an amazing view in all directions."

To their left, they could see the summit towering above the pines they had just walked through, then behind it the sheltered bay they had just climbed up from leading out into Queen Charlotte Sound, with a number of boats passing by. Opposite them was Arapawa Island, and Tom pointed out Captain Cook's lookout at the top of the highest peak, from which Cook discovered the shortcut that became known as Tory Channel. Further to the right, they could see the entrance to Tory Channel, with a freight ferry making its way towards Picton. Directly in front of them was the point itself and the entrance to the Bay of Many Coves, which, true to its name, was characterized by a number of concealed coves, each of which had a sprinkling of baches, boathouses, and associated jetties.

After they had all taken photos of this stunning panorama, Tom brought them down to earth with the fact that the path to the left led directly down to the bach behind the pohutukawa, where the Shannons had seen the suspicious men arriving. He reminded them that it was relatively easy for the new arrivals to climb up from their bach onto the ridge and walk up the ridge track past their property.

"In fact, they might have been up here already," he added.

They then walked back through the pines and past the clearing at the top of the property and were just starting the long haul up what seemed like an almost vertical track to the summit when there was another gunshot, much closer this time.

Luise was quite shocked. "*Mein Gott*! That sounded like it was coming from the top of this track!"

All three of them scrambled behind a large pine tree. Luise cautiously peered out from behind the tree and looked up the track. As she did, a figure appeared at the top of the track, silhouetted against the sky.

"Oh no! He's got a rifle, and he's aiming it at us!"

CHAPTER 9

"Hoy! Is that someone down there?"

Luise took another peek out from behind the tree and saw that he had lowered his rifle.

"Yes, there's three of us here!"

"Sorry about that. I thought I had heard a goat in the bushes," the rifleman called down to them. "I'm out goat hunting. Those goats are such a nuisance. They create havoc wherever they go."

He started walking down the hill towards them, his rifle down and pointed well away from them. Luise felt it was now safe enough for them to emerge from their refuge, and the others followed her out. The rifleman approached them with his hand out, ready to shake hands.

"Hi, I'm Ryan Scott. I live in Milton Bay, just a bit further along the track. Sorry to give you such a fright." Tom introduced him to Luise and Jake and explained that they were all staying at Innisfree.

"Ah yes, Tom, I think I met you years ago when you were a little toddler. I wouldn't have been much older. I reckon your parents know my parents. So your guests are from Germany and the United States? Never been here before? Well, if you've got a few minutes, let me show you a bit of Milton Bay."

The trio was happy to do so and followed him up the hill to the summit, where they stopped for a while to admire the view.

"I call this the best view in the world," said Ryan.

"Well, it is stunning," Jake conceded. "It's almost as good as the view from the top of Cathedral Mountain."

"He's talking about the Glass Mountains in Oklahoma," Tom explained to Ryan. "That's a completely different view, a view of mesas over the prairie. This is a sea view of islands, bays, and channels, like fiords. Amazing, with Snake Point in front of us, leading down to the sea, and way in the distance, you can make out Picton. And it's so quiet!"

They all took photos of the panorama and soaked in what Ryan called the "unique atmosphere" of the summit. It was completely quiet apart from the distant buzzing of insects, which, from their recent experience of Lake Stechlin omens, they assumed were dragonflies, coming from further towards the point.

Ryan then led them along a little path down the other side of the hill, which wound its way through dense pine trees until they could glimpse the sea glimmering through the trees. Then as they entered a clearing, the Bay of Many Coves opened up before them, and below them, they saw a beach with a number of jetties.

"Welcome to Milton Bay!" said Ryan. "That's our place over there," he said, pointing to a large white cottage with a verandah overlooking the lawn and a meticulously kept garden. "See that flat patch over there to the right of the cottage? My dad designed that as a helipad! I think we've only ever used it once when the prime minister came over for a book launch. But still, it's good for emergency use."

He took them over to the jetty. As they were standing there, Luise spotted to her left what looked like two large fish approaching. Then a large grey nose suddenly appeared out of the water, followed by big eyes and a sleek, smooth grey body with fins, which splashed down in front of her, followed by another.

Luise pointed excitedly to the left of the jetty. "*Mein Gott! Delfine!*"

"Yes, dolphins!" shouted Tom. They all looked out to the left and discovered there was a whole group of dolphins, or a pod, coming over to the jetty. They were swimming under water and surfacing briefly for air, splashing down playfully in front of the jetty and looking up at them.

"We get a lot of dolphins around the Bay of Many Coves," Ryan told them. "When they see you on the jetty, they often want to come over and say hello."

"Yes. I remember last time I left Innisfree, the dolphins that had come over to say hello accompanied the local ferry that collected me all the way to the point, putting on such a lovely display—as if to say, 'Come back soon!'" said Tom.

Luise and Jake were utterly spellbound by the spectacle of the dolphins swimming around and around the jetty, splashing around playfully and looking up at them as if they wanted to welcome them.

"I've never seen anything like this before. One thing we don't have in Oklahoma is dolphins." Jake smiled, taking lots of photos and videos for his friends.

They could have watched the dolphins all afternoon, but they realized they had to get back, so thanked Ryan for his support.

"If you ever need any help, let me know. You know where to find me."

"Well, actually, there have been strange things happening on our side of Snake Point," said Tom. "Ray Shannon said she had seen people with guns arriving at the bach between hers and ours. I thought they might have been after the goats. When we heard your gunshots, we thought it must have been them."

"I see. Doesn't sound too good. Let's swap numbers, then. If there's anything I can do, let me know. Ryan Scott at your service!"

The dolphin display, together with Ryan's generosity, made the ascent back up the hill an easy climb, and they were all in an ebullient mood as they reached the clearing that led to the track back down the hill to Innisfree. They were just about to make their way back past the toetoe and gorse to the group of pine trees at the top of the track when Jake remembered something.

"Hey, Tom, what about the message bottle Ray Shannon told us about? Is it still here?"

"Yes, I always leave a message in it whenever I'm visiting. Practically everyone that comes up on the ridge leaves a message. It's an old tradition."

They returned to the ridge track and walked a short way down the avenue of pine trees until Tom abruptly turned to the right. Attached to the third tree back was an old plastic milk bottle slit down the front, with a number of pieces of paper and a pencil inside. These looked as if they had been there for some time.

Tom pulled out one that he recognized. "This is a page from my old diary that I update every time I come up here. Look, last February. Just before the university went back. And look, my cousins were here just the following week. Let's add our names."

All three of them added their names and

signatures, and at Luise's suggestion, they added "Glass Mountains Mission" at the end. "No one will ever know what that means, but that's what we're here for," she added.

"Some of them mention walking right down to the point and back," said Jake, reading through the notes. "How easy is it to do that, Tom? Can we get down to the point this afternoon?"

"Good idea. But let's have lunch first."

They headed back to the clearing and down the steep track, slipping and sliding as they went and grabbing hold of any manuka branch or trunk they could find to break their fall. They had sardines on toast for lunch, then had a relaxing time just enjoying the view from the cabin verandah. Luise noticed what she thought was birds splashing in the water just out from the jetty, then, deciding to check it out with the binoculars, discovered it was a group of dolphins. She ran down to the jetty, closely followed by the others, and waved and called out to the dolphins from the end of the wharf. Sure enough, they came over to her and circled round the jetty, looking up at her as they jumped out of the water, each one seemingly trying to outdo the other in their leaps and splashdowns.

Luise stood there, enthralled. "Such friendliness! We are guests of nature here — *Gast der Natur* — but I've never seen such a wonderful display of hospitality from nature as this. *Wunderbar!*"

After a few minutes of swimming and splashing, which the dolphins seemed to be enjoying as much as their audience of three, one of the dolphins headed off towards the point, and the others followed, past the boatshed and along the beach.

"I used to have races with them along the foreshore," Tom recalled. "But they always won."

They all looked intently down the beach as the dolphins disappeared into the distance, and then they noticed something unusual.

"What's that around the pohutukawa tree? A swarm of insects?" Jake asked.

They all gazed attentively at the pohutukawa tree in the distance. Jake was right. There seemed to be a massive cloud of swarming insects above the pohutukawa. As they watched, the cloud of insects started moving up the coast towards them, following the beach that separated the boathouse from the pohutukawa and hovering over each pine tree that had fallen over the sand. The insects soon reached the boatshed, and they swarmed above the roof for several minutes, flying around and around and in and out for no apparent reason but keeping within their cluster, as if they were a flock of birds.

Tom decided to go over to the boatshed to see if he could work out what sort of insects they were. Luise and Jake stayed on the jetty, taking videos, as they thought that videos of this, together with the dolphins, would be a big hit on the Internet. When Tom came back, he told them the insects were definitely dragonflies and that the buzzing noise was deafening, like the dragonflies at Lake Stechlin.

Just as he said that, the cloud of insects started moving, heading back, slowly but surely, in the direction they had come from, pausing over each fallen pine tree, then swarming over the pohutukawa before they dispersed into the trees behind.

"Well! Talk about the Atafu omen," said Tom. "I wonder what Lake Stechlin is trying to tell us?"

Luise suggested that seeing it was all in the realm of speculation, they should go ahead with their plan to go back up on the ridge and head down to the point along the ridge track. "Who knows, perhaps we will see something up there."

Jake and Tom thought that was a good idea, and after walking up the three-hundred-and-eighty zig-zag steps to the bach, Luise and Luke took some bottles of water for the remaining fourteen-hundred steps, realizing now that the climb was just as precipitous and exhausting as Tom had said it would be. They followed Tom once again, grabbing hold of each manuka branch they could find to propel themselves upwards. It did not take quite as long the second time around, and when they reached the top, they were happy to simply keep going down the ridge track through the pines, as this bit was downhill.

"We've got the American University Eagles behind us — this bit is Sacred Heart," Jake chuckled. He did not explain further, but it was clear he was referring to university wrestling teams he had encountered. They passed what Jake called the crocodile house, with its large window panels, and Tom pointed out a track just before it that would go directly down to the pohutukawa bach. The ridge track took them past two more houses before disappearing into some native bush and emerging at a large tennis court. Tom told them they had better stop there, as they were now entering private property, so they took shots of the extensive views of the Bay of Many Coves on one side and Queen Charlotte Sound on the other, and Tom pointed out the resort opposite, where the local ferry had called in on their way to Innisfree. They made their way back up the track, which Jake christened Grand View, though the others were not quite sure whether he was referring to the view or another university wrestling team he had encountered.

Just before they reached the top of the steep track down to Innisfree, Jake glanced at the message bottle and thought he noticed something different. On closer inspection, he discovered that in front of the old message notes, including those they had contributed to, there was a new sheet of paper, looking very clean and white.

"Hey, guys, there's a new message in there.

Let's take a look."

He opened up the side of the bottle and unfolded the piece of paper. He looked thunderstruck as he read it. The others rushed up to him. They could not believe what they were reading.

We know where you are.

CHAPTER 10

"We know where you are," Jake repeated. "And today's date. For crying out loud. They're here! And they know about us!"

"But how would they have known about the message bottle?" Luise asked.

"From a local," Tom ventured. "They couldn't have gotten up to the ridge track by themselves. They must have someone with them who has lived here. He would know how people always leave messages in the bottle."

Luise pulled a face. "So perhaps we shouldn't have mentioned the Glass Mountains Mission in our message, after all, Tom?"

"Well, I expect it only confirmed what they already knew. But it's a bit spooky. When did they come up here? Where are they now? They could be anywhere around here. Hiding behind the trees. Anywhere."

"They must have come up here while we were down with the dolphins," said Jake.

"Ah yes, while we were watching the dolphins. That explains all the dragonflies. They came over to warn us. Just like they did at Lake Stechlin."

"Didn't you say in Fontane's novel it's the lake that warns the characters to be on their guard, Tom?"

"Yes, I think it's very similar to that, Jake. A Fontane prefiguration."

Luise was quite excited at this idea. "A Fontane prefiguration and an Atafu omen combined! Well, I think we're more than guests of nature here. Nature's looking after us."

"Well, in a way, you're right," said Tom. "I sometimes reckon the friendly wekas around here are a bit like guard dogs. They screech when strangers are approaching."

Realizing that someone could be hiding near them on the ridge track and might overhear them, they decided they should return to the bach to discuss any further action. They slipped and slid down the track in record time, now that they had been able to familiarize themselves with the best manuka branches to grab on the way down. Once back in the bach, they unanimously decided to get Robert Shannon involved. Tom sent him a message about what they had found. Robert replied immediately, saying he would go up through the pine forest and hide at a point on their boundary overlooking their bach to see what he could find out.

In the meantime, the trio returned to writing their manifesto. They decided they needed to express the main arguments in their manifesto in clear language that everyone would understand.

"No more divisiveness. We must work together. Common sense. The main point is: Get rid of that revenge mentality," Jake emphasized.

"How can we say that succinctly, then?" asked Tom.

"How about Rise above revenge? Does that work in English?" Luise suggested.

"Rise above revenge—R.A.R. Perfect! Let's make that our motto, don't you think, Jake?"

"You betcha!"

Then there was a buzz from Tom's phone. Tom grabbed it straight away to find a message from Robert. Tom read it out loud.

"They've been talking about you. One local, two Americans. One with glasses, the other with a beard. Planning to ambush you via ridge track. Just setting off. They'll be heading down to your place from the ridge, but local says he hasn't been that way for years. Can't see any rifles. Reckon they just want to give you a fright."

"Well, we know who they are. Pasty Face and Beardy Weirdy," Jake laughed.

"Yes, but this is serious. We know why they're here. To stop us. And we know what they're capable of," warned Luise, rubbing her shoulder.

"And apart from getting us out of the way, do you think they are aiming to get at our manifesto too by pinching all our electronic gear? I bet that's it. Where's the best place to hide it, Tom?"

Tom showed them a hidden recess underneath the bach where keys were held. "They'll never find them there."

They decided all three of them should be sitting where they would be easily seen from above, just looking harmless, with Jake closest to the track they would be coming down. He could get one into a wrestling hold while Tom and Luise overpowered the others.

"I reckon I've got enough time to teach you two the basics of the high single-leg takedown," said Jake. "That'll take care of them."

Tom then texted Robert that they were prepared.

Jake demonstrated on Tom exactly what a single leg takedown involved. Luise made sure her left shoulder was up to it, then tried out the technique on both Jake and Tom, with great success.

"*Mein Gott*! I never would have thought I could be a wrestler. This is fun! In German, it's called 'Ringen.' We'll run rings around these three!"

They were in the middle of perfecting their

wrestling moves on each other when there was an almighty screech from a weka just next to the cabin. They all looked up, startled, and then turned in the direction the weka was facing. They moved off the verandah and looked up the hill. Was there someone up on the ridge?

"Listen," Tom hissed. In the distance, they could hear some twigs snapping.

"That must be them," said Luise. "And look over there! There's a cloud of dragonflies heading right up to the ridge. Lake Stechlin dragonflies! They're warning us too! *Erstaunlich*! Amazing!"

They listened intently. The sound of twigs snapping then changed to the sound of broken foliage, thumping, and sliding.

"They're getting to the steep bit!" Jake whispered.

Suddenly there was an enormous thump and the sound of broken branches, followed by a massive screeching yell.

"Faaaark! I've broken my leg!"

They decided they had better go up and see what was going on and help if necessary. Whoever had fallen sounded like he was in utter agony. By the time they got to the spot where it was obvious someone had slipped, no one was to be seen, but as they approached the ridge, they could see two figures through the trees dragging a third man up to the ridge and then supporting him back along the ridge track. Because the dragonflies were making such a noise, it was difficult to hear what they were saying, but they certainly heard the injured man complaining bitterly about the steep track and saying he would never go down there again. No one should, he said.

"They obviously don't know you have to swing your way through by grabbing the manuka branches," said Tom. "Nothing else will take your weight. I've slipped so many times on that track. The old punga tree ferns just break off at the base. The flax pulls out, and no one wants to grab cutty grass. It's only the manuka that takes your weight."

They decided to head back to the bach, carefully negotiating their way down via the manuka trees and branches. After making sure their electronic gear was still safely stowed away, they walked down to the jetty. Luise suggested they would get a better view from there on what might now be going on behind the pohutukawa tree. Luise stood at the end of the jetty while the others opened up the boatshed. When they joined Luise, she was excitedly pointing into the water.

"What's that? It looks like some sort of mythical animal with massive wings trying to fly under water."

It was a large, flat, grey creature about four feet long, propelling itself along quite gracefully in the water with what looked like large wings about two feet in length.

Tom looked carefully. "That's a stingray. You have to watch out for them when you're in the water. It's not called a stingray for nothing. The tail is venomous, and its sting is incredibly painful. But it'll only sting you if you step on it. The rest of the time, they're just nice to look at."

"I've never seen anything like that before," said Luise. "We certainly don't have anything like that in Berlin or Brandenburg. What about Oklahoma, Jake?"

"No way, nothing like that in Oklahoma either. We don't even have a sea!"

Jake and Luise were busily taking photos of the stingray and various jellyfish that ventured close to the jetty when Tom noticed some dolphins.

Luise looked up. "*Delfine!*"

Tom was pointing towards Arapawa Island. Sure enough, there was a group of dolphins halfway across the channel, leaping and diving and generally having a great time splashing around. Luise waved to them, and amazingly, they again came over to the jetty and swam around in circles in front of them as if to say hello.

Luise was elated. "What lovely, friendly creatures!" There were six dolphins diving in unison into the water, swimming along just below water level, then emerging and leaping up into the air, and she could see their eyes looking at her as they paused momentarily before they dived back in again, swimming around in large circles. Luise took out her phone and took a video of what she referred to in her commentary as *her* dolphins — *meine Delfine*. The dolphins kept up their performance for a number of minutes, then moved back out into the channel.

It was then that they noticed a boat approaching the pohutukawa tree further down the point. Tom thought it looked like the water taxi that was stationed at the Bay of Many Coves. At the same time, a swarm of insects was making its way to the pohutukawa tree.

"What are those dragonflies trying to tell us?" Jake dashed over to the boatshed to get the binoculars and ran back to the jetty, focussing them on the pohutukawa tree. "It's Pasty Face! He's been injured. Look! The other two are carrying him over to the boat!"

Luise and Tom took turns looking through the binoculars. They saw the skipper take the boat as far up the beach as he could, then he got out to help lift the injured man into the boat. The man supporting Pasty Face's shoulders looked very much like the Beardy Weirdy they remembered from Lake Stechlin. The other man, carrying him by his legs, was thin, tall, and lanky, whereas Beardy Weirdy was well built, muscular, and looked fit.

"If he was a wrestler, he'd be a 184-pounder," commented Jake, focussing on him through the binoculars. "I don't think he is, though. Wrestling's not so popular in California. Maybe football."

The skipper appeared to be asking them questions and was relaying their replies into his radio phone.

"It looks like he's asking them for some ID or something," said Jake.

Then Beardy Weirdy hopped out of the boat and pushed it back into the water, while the tall man, who they decided to christen Cranky Lanky, sat in the boat with Pasty Face as the skipper negotiated his way past the rocks and into the channel. Beardy Weirdy stood on the beach, watching the boat disappear past the point in the direction of Picton. Then he walked back towards the pohutukawa and went out of sight.

Just as Beardy Weirdy disappeared from view, Tom's phone buzzed with a text from Robert.

"He's got a broken leg. Taking him to hospital. Been listening to them. Next time just one person is coming. Along the beach this time. With a gun. Will come down by kayak to tell you more when the coast is clear."

"Well!" said Luise. "Stingrays and dolphins. We know who the stingrays are. Beardy Weirdy, Pasty Face, Cranky Lanky. Robert has the spirit of the dolphins."

"Salt of the earth, my dad would say. Matthew 5:13," Jake agreed.

Jake and Tom decided to head back up to the bach to see if they could finalize their work on the manifesto, seeing they now had a bit of time. Luise said she would go for a little walk down the beach to see if she could find any more marine life.

"Okay, Luise, but watch out for stingrays."

"Don't worry, Tom, I will. I know what they look like now."

Luise walked around the back of the boatshed to the beach beyond. She made her way along the beach, clambered over a number of fallen branches, carefully negotiated her way along the rocks covered with mussels, and was approaching a large pine tree when she heard a grunting noise from behind the tree. She stopped in her tracks. Was that someone hiding behind the tree?

CHAPTER 11

Luise approached the tree gingerly and inched her way around it. Then suddenly, she was confronted with two eyes, exactly level with hers. She got such a fright she jumped back and then realized that it was not a person. Was it a dog? He had a pointed nose like a dog and long whiskers pointing downwards on either side of his mouth. He had two tiny ears that poked out of his head like little horns. His big brown eyes peered at her intently in a quizzical fashion. For a moment, Luise was convinced that the three new arrivals had brought a dog with them, in which case she was sure Tom would have a name for him. Doggy Woggy, perhaps? Then she looked down. Flippers!

Ein Seelöwe! A *sea lion*! she thought.

Just at that moment, the creature flopped down in front of her and started pulling himself up the rocks with his front flippers, and then hopped from rock to rock, waddling off until he reached the sea, where he dived into the water. She watched him as he swam down in the direction of the pohutukawa tree, then came back to shore, dragged himself up onto a large rock, and seemed to be gazing intently towards a clump of trees between the rocks and the bank. Luise followed his gaze and moved over the rocks to the trees he was looking at. "*Ach so!*" she said to herself. "I see! A perfect place for an ambush."

She remembered how, when they were waiting for what they thought was a gun-toting villain coming up the track behind them at the Glass Mountains, they had worked out a strategy whereby Tom would disarm him by means of a point fieldsman cricket throw from a concealed spot behind a tree, after which Jake would tackle him in a high-speed single leg takedown and immobilize him. This was the perfect spot for a repeat performance!

She turned to the sea lion, waved, and thanked him. "*Danke!*" He raised his front flipper as if to wave back and dragged himself back down the rock, and flopped into the water. *Well, if Lake Stechlin had anything to do with this, it is certainly looking after us,* Luise thought as she started clambering back over the rocks to the boatshed. "*Schöne Tiere!* Nice animals! Nice dolphins, nice sea lions around here. Pity about the stingray."

Luise passed behind the boatshed and then made her way back up the zigzag to the bach, where she found Jake and Tom still working on the manifesto.

"Guess what! I met a sea lion!"

Luise proceeded to tell them in great detail about her encounter with the sea lion and what she had discovered in the process.

"Hey, that's pretty exciting! And a sea lion called Doggy Woggy," Tom laughed. "It won't be a real sea lion, though. It'll be a fur seal. Looks just like a sea lion but has a more pointed nose and drags itself along instead of walking on all fours. They like rocky beaches, so you see quite a lot of them around the sounds. I've noticed that when Germans on the ferry see fur seals, they always refer to them as '*Seelöwen*,' sea lions. Whatever, let's go down and see what our Doggy Woggy has found for us."

"From what you say, it sounds like the perfect place for an ambush," said Jake. "I'm assuming it'll be Beardy Weirdy because Cranky Lanky would be a pushover. I'd better train up for a high single-leg takedown on this 184-pounder. Well, I'm used to 197-pounders, so if we time it right, we should be fine."

All three went down the zig-zag to the beach, and Luise led them down past the boatshed and over the rocks and fallen trees to the clearing she had found with the help of her sea lion friend. There was a patch of sand between two groups of rocks, and to the right of the patch of sand, and extending beyond the sand to the next line of rocks, were a number of trees.

"That's perfect!" said Jake. "I need level ground for when I tackle him with my high single-leg takedown and sand for him to fall on so I can immobilize him. Now, Tom, we'll need your point fieldsman cricketer skills to disarm him first. You'll need to hide behind a tree so he can't see you, just as we did on Cathedral Mountain, and then as soon as he produces his gun, you aim for that hand with a rock and disarm him. Then at that moment, I'll dive for his leg and bring him down. I can get him down in two seconds. Once he's immobilized, you can come over and help. Then we'll have to let Robert know. Luise, you and I will need to be chatting as if nothing is going on, so he won't suspect anything as he approaches. Then when he produces his gun, our plan comes into action. Luise, once he's under control, you will need to grab his gun and call Robert to tell him what's going on."

At this, Tom searched around for a suitable rock and eventually found one that was the right size. He then tried aiming it into various parts of the clearing so he could familiarize himself with its performance. He was satisfied that this one would do the trick and put it in his pocket. Then he asked Jake to walk through the clearing several times while he hid behind the tree and took aim. Jake had to make sure Tom was not visible at any stage. Tom then showed Luise and Jake where they needed to stand for maximum impact. Luise and Jake decided they would pretend to be observing the bird life. They would then greet the stranger in a friendly manner. "Just like we did when we were waiting for the guy in the Dodge to come up the Cathedral Mountain track."

"On that occasion, he turned out to be the Glass Mountains ranger, Brent Lehman, and he was fine," said Luise. "But nothing like that this time. This is the real thing. And we know what he's capable of."

"Yes, he will stop at nothing. But we have to look as relaxed and friendly as possible, so he doesn't suspect anything. We're friendly Oklahomans again. Or friendly Kiwis, if you like. We must not let on that we recognize him or know who he is. So we will need to say something like, 'Hi! Great bird life around here this time of the evening.' Then presumably he produces his gun, Tom disarms him, I go for his upper right leg and bring him down, and Luise, you grab his gun."

They rehearsed this scenario a number of times until they were happy that each person knew exactly what to do at any particular moment. Then just as they were about to head back to the boatshed, Luise noticed a familiar face in the rocks.

"*Mein Seelöwe*! My sea lion! Look!"

They all looked over to where Luise was pointing, and sure enough, a fur seal was sitting on a rock, observing them intently.

Tom laughed. "So that's Doggy Woggy!" They all waved at him, at which he lifted his front flipper as if to wave back, then pulled himself around and plopped back into the water as if he was now content with a job well done.

They happily made their way back to the boatshed and up to the bach, where they decided to have a well-earned dinner. They had just finished their dessert of tinned apricots and corn flakes when they noticed that Robert had arrived at the jetty and was waving up at them. All three ran down the zig-zag to hear the latest news.

"Well," said Robert, as they all sat down on the lawn facing the jetty, "I've got quite a lot to report. We know the water taxi skipper that collected the guy with the broken leg, and he tells me they all had to produce IDs because it was an official rescue operation to get him to the Emergency Department of Wairau Hospital in Blenheim. The American guy with glasses that broke his leg is Cortland Heller, the tall New Zealander that went with him is Doug Clagon, and the bearded American that stayed behind is Zachary Swaber."

"So our Beardy Weirdy is Zach," Jake laughed. "And Pasty Face is Cortland, you said? And the guy with the local knowledge—we call him Cranky Lanky—is Doug?"

"That would be right, and I have been listening to them talking," Robert went on. "They have it in for you for some reason. But they don't want to attempt the ridge track access again. Doug has suggested that just one of them should go and along the beach this time. He is saying they should leave it till tomorrow evening when it's low tide. He's told them about the zig-zag track up the hill from the other side of the boatshed. Well, with Cortland out of the way in hospital, that just leaves Zach. I don't know if Doug will be back by tomorrow night, but even if he is, it'll be Zach heading your way tomorrow evening. But this time, the crucial thing is he'll have a gun."

"Thanks for all that," said Tom, "and for your text. Since we got it, we've been working out the best way to ambush him as he walks along the beach. What we need to know is, when is he going to set out? We can be in the general area from late afternoon, but we need to be in position as soon as he sets out."

"Well, I can be on sentry duty in the bush right next to their bach, and I can text you as soon as he sets out. And can you text me as soon as you have him under control?"

"Yes, I can do that. That's my job," said Luise.

"Good, then I can alert the authorities. The thing is, they haven't done anything illegal yet. But if he threatens you with a gun, we have to call the police. So you're planning to ambush him? How—

and where?"

Jake, Tom, and Luise took Robert along the beach to the clearing where they had been practicing the ambush. They got Robert to approach them as if he had a pistol in his hand, showed him how Tom was going to disarm him, and then Jake demonstrated the single leg takedown maneuver, bringing him gently down onto the sand, and Luise showed how she then had to grab the pistol and text Robert as to what had happened.

Robert was very impressed. "Your text needs to be a very brief one, seeing I now know exactly what is going to happen. Then I can swing into action. What can you text me?"

"Well, we like to call ourselves a mission. So what about 'mission successful'?"

"Right-oh. And if it's not?"

"If it's not, I won't be texting you! You had better alert the authorities half an hour after you see him leave because we could be in trouble."

"Yes, absolutely. We mustn't get too smug," Tom agreed. "These are desperate people. They have no principles, and we know they don't shrink from violence. Didn't you say they arrived with rifles and ammunition, Robert?"

"They did, but I reckon that was for their earlier plan that they had to abandon after Cortland broke his leg. Zach won't have a rifle."

"You betcha," Jake agreed. "If Zach is going to be clambering over rocks and then up the hill, he won't be carrying a rifle. That's too cumbersome. No American would ever do that. He'll have a pistol in his jacket pocket. That's what we're prepared for."

At that, they rehearsed their moves again with Robert, who remarked that he would like to learn more wrestling moves, as they would help him with his rugby. Then they walked back to the boatshed, where Robert put on his life jacket and hopped back into his kayak.

"Tom, I'll send you a brief text tomorrow as soon as he leaves. It'll be 'Off now.' I'll wait for your text, Luise, a few minutes later, and then I'll do my bit."

"*Wunderbar!*" Luise smiled. "Let's hope it's 'mission successful.'"

CHAPTER 12

"Low tide is due at 6.30 p.m., so I reckon we should be down on the beach at 5.30 p.m. to get ourselves into position as soon as we get word from Robert," Tom suggested as they sat down to relax after lunch. The trio had spent the morning putting the finishing touches on the Glass Mountains Manifesto and decided it was now in the sort of format that Patrick McBryde had had in mind when he proposed that they could meet up with the CNN crew at the Glass Mountains to launch their manifesto. Having gotten the manifesto into shape, they felt they could now concentrate on the immediate challenge of how to deal with Zachary Swaber—or, as they preferred to call him, Beardy Weirdy. They realized that total preparedness was absolutely crucial, as things could easily go wrong, and if they did, the consequences could be fatal.

"Yes, 5.30 is a good time," Jake agreed. "We don't

want to be seen hanging around the wharf at 6.30, or Beardy might change his mind. He is expecting us to be up the hill in the bach. We need to be on the rocks at the back of the beach next to our ambush point so we won't be seen from their pohutukawa bay. Then we can move to our positions as soon as Robert texts you, Tom."

They spent the afternoon tidying up and getting things ready for a possible departure the following day. Tom had been in touch with his uncle Bill in Wellington to see if a direct flight from Auckland to Houston, Texas, might be feasible over the next few days. From there, they would be able to fly to Oklahoma City and hopefully be able to find a cottage at the Sooner Suites on the University of Oklahoma campus, which they could use as their base for the Glass Mountains Manifesto launch. It all sounded quite exciting, but they were under no illusions as to the fragility of their present situation. Things could go wrong at any moment, seriously wrong.

At 5.15 p.m., they locked everything up and walked down the zig-zag to the jetty and from there moved along the bottom of the cliff behind the boatshed so they would not be seen from further down the point. By five-thirty, they had found some suitable rocks to sit on, right next to the sandy clearing where they planned to stage their ambush.

"Well, seeing you two are about to show off

your cricket and wrestling expertise, how about a yoga exercise?" Luise asked.

"How about the one you taught us on the Glass Mountains?"

"*Ach ja*! The vertical eye movement exercise. *Netra vyayamam*. It helps concentration. Do you remember how to do it? You stand straight like this, with your head facing straight ahead and your hands tightly clasped in front of you. Then you keep your head in position and move your eyes to look down as far as you can, and breathe in slowly as you move your eyes up as far as they will go. You then close your eyes, breathe out slowly, keeping your eyes in that position, then relax your hands and open your eyes. Let's do it now."

Jake and Tom remembered how useful the exercise had been at a critical time on the Glass Mountains and were happy to do it again. They followed Luise's instructions, breathed out slowly, and all opened their eyes at the same time. They were fascinated by the beauty of the scene which lay before them. The whole of Arapawa Island on the other side of Queen Charlotte Sound was bathed in the beautiful red color of the sun that was sinking behind them, while ripples all the way across the sea glistened in the warm glow of the setting sun as if to reassure them that all was well. It was so still that all they could hear was water gently lapping against the rocks.

"What a beautiful, peaceful sunset," Tom remarked. "As if nothing could go wrong. But if we were in a novel by Fontane, this sunset would be a precursor of doom."

"Well, we are in charge," said Jake. "We can overcome all the challenges that will confront us. It's a matter of managing them properly, and that's what we will do, don't you think, Luise?"

"Yes, the Netra vyayamam exercise helps concentration and intellectual response. It will help the three of us to deal with anything we are confronted with over the next few minutes. *Selbstvertrauen*. Self-confidence. That's what it's all about."

A shag flew overhead and landed on the boat ramp in front of the boathouse. As it started to preen itself, they noticed that the surface of the water just beyond it was starting to shimmer, and then to Luise's delight, they caught sight of a dolphin heading their way. It came right up to the rocks, seemed to look at them, and swam up and down the beach as if it was daring them to come and have a race. It then leapt up in the air, splashed into the sea, and leapt up again to do a somersault. The three of them were so taken by the dolphin's antics that they would have gone down to play with him were it not for the fact that they realized they must not draw attention to themselves. The dolphin swirled around several times, gave them a farewell somersault, and headed off towards the pohutukawa.

"All we need now is Doggy Woggy!" Tom joked. But as they looked at the pohutukawa, they noticed a large swarm of insects above it. Then they started to move towards them. "Dragonflies! Listen to them droning. Lake Stechlin again. It's the Atafu omen! He must be on his way!"

There was a loud screeching sound from a weka behind them.

"The weka's warning us," said Jake. "Time to get into our positions!"

They wasted no time in getting into the configuration they had rehearsed so well. Tom hid behind the tree while Luise and Jake moved out into the clearing and stood on the patch of sand. Just at that moment, Tom received a text from Robert. "'Off now.'"

"Beardy's on his way," he hissed to the others. He put his phone away and took the rock out of his pocket. Looking through a little gap in the leaves, he then spied Beardy Weirdy coming into view, climbing over the rocks at the entrance to the bay. He tightened his grip on the rock and imagined it was a cricket ball. He remembered that he was coached to aim at the base of the stump. This time the stump was the pistol that Beardy would be carrying.

Jake and Luise saw Beardy as well but pretended this newcomer was nothing out of the ordinary, given that the coast was public land. They continued to observe the waves and the seagulls and talked to each other about the various techniques the seagulls were using to dive for their prey. As Beardy negotiated the last row of rocks before the sandy clearing, they simply glanced at him with a brief smile and turned their attention back to the seagulls. Last time, Jake had reminded Luise, when they were in a similar situation on Cathedral Mountain, they had to be nice Oklahomans, and this time they needed to be friendly New Zealanders. But they must not let on that they recognized him.

"Great bird life round here this time of the evening," said Jake, acknowledging Beardy as he approached.

Beardy did not reply. He resolutely looked at Jake and Luise as he walked towards them. Jake stared at him intently, assessing how best to tackle him. He focused on his upper right thigh, as that would be his point of attack, and he felt his adrenalin levels rise as they did when he was about to carry out a move on a wrestling opponent. As with a wrestling move, so much depended on the element of surprise. He needed to catch Beardy off guard, and if things went according to plan, that opportunity would come within the next few seconds.

As soon as Beardy was clear of the rocks, he walked up to Jake and Luise and stopped about two meters away from them. He then reached into his pocket and, as they expected, produced a pistol, which he aimed steadily at Jake. Jake and Luise ceased their friendly banter and stared at Beardy as if they were shocked and completely frozen.

At that moment, Tom prepared to throw a direct shot from behind the tree. He imagined he was a point fieldsman aiming directly at the base of the stump. It had to be a flat throw — a fast, direct, and straight throw. He let fly, and it was a perfect hit. It hit Beardy's right hand with considerable severity, so the pistol flew out of Beardy's hand and landed on the rocks next to him.

As Beardy was looking around to see where his pistol had landed, Jake jumped forward and lunged with both hands, his left hand moving between Beardy's legs and joining his right hand around the back of his upper right thigh enabling Jake to tug him forwards. With his head now down at Beardy's waist, he pulled Beardy's leg upwards and put his left leg behind Beardy's other leg and jerked it forward, causing Beardy to lose balance and fall backwards. As he fell, Jake put his left hand behind Beardy's shoulder, then moved his other hand up behind Beardy's back, breaking his fall as he dropped backwards onto the sand.

Jake kept his right arm in place while he moved his left arm under Beardy's right arm, putting all his weight on Beardy's upper body from right to left, his legs digging into the sand to give him extra strength and traction. Beardy was pinned, unable to move, though struggling to free himself by lifting his knees up and kicking his legs around in the air. It was all over within five seconds.

Luise immediately grabbed the pistol from between the rocks where it had landed and put it safely in her backpack. As she did this, Tom ran over to help Jake subdue Beardy by sitting on his legs. Now he did not have a chance of getting up. Luise took out her smartphone and texted Robert. *Mission successful.*

"Well done, Tom! Perfect point fieldsman shot!" said Jake.

"And your high single leg takedown worked perfectly!" responded Tom.

Then, turning to Beardy, Jake asked, "Why did you do this? Why the gun?"

"Well, someone has to stop you," Beardy gasped.

"Why?"

"You're so naïve. The world can't survive without armies and troops."

"Well, our New Zealand troops don't engage in war," said Tom. "We use our troops for training and international peacekeeping."

"A small country might be able to do that, but what about big countries like the U.S., China, and

Russia? We have to stop you. And now. You might have won this battle, but there will be more to come. And if we can't stop you here, we'll stop you—"

Beardy's words were drowned out by an ear-splitting booming noise that came from just above them.

CHAPTER 13

They immediately looked up above them. The booming noise turned into a deafening chopping sound, and they became aware of a helicopter which had come over the ridge and was now hovering just above them.

"It's a police helicopter!" Tom shouted. "Where did that come from? Hang on, Jake, can you take care of our friend here? I'll direct them to a landing site by the boatshed."

"You betcha," Jake responded, putting more weight on Beardy's chest and tightening his grip on Beardy's upper back.

Tom jumped up, scrambled over the rocks, and ran down the beach to the boatshed. Ducking under the boat ramp, as it was low tide, he pointed to the freshly mown tent site where the helicopter could land. The pilot gave it a thumbs up, maneuvered the helicopter into position, and landed it safely. As soon as it had touched down, two armed police hopped out of the left hand door and ran over to Tom.

"Where is he?" said one.

"He's over there. He's still pinned to the ground. Jake got him down with a single leg wrestling move, and he hasn't budged since. "

"Good stuff! Where's his gun?"

"Luise's got his gun. It's in her backpack."

"How did you get his gun off him?"

"I disarmed him with a point fieldsman throw."

"Ah! A cricketer like me! Good man!"

At that, the two armed policemen made their way over to the scene of the confrontation, where they produced their rifles, told Beardy that he was under arrest, and asked him to stand up with his arms raised. Jake released him carefully and stood by Luise while Beardy stood up and was marched off to the helicopter. Once he was safely inside, one of them came back to retrieve the pistol from Luise.

"You three have done an excellent job," he said. "Fantastic teamwork. I'll need to come back later to get statements from you. But in the meantime, is there anything else we should know?"

"I think there is a third person involved," said Tom. "Three of them tried to come down our track from the ridge, and one, Cortland, broke his leg, so they gave up. This guy's name is Zach. There's a third guy called Doug, who seems to be a local."

"And he's at the bach behind the pohutukawa over there?"

"Yes, that's right."

"Good. I know the one. He's now back at the bach. We saw him from the helicopter. I'll talk to him when I come back in the police launch. How do you know their names?"

"From the skipper of the water taxi that collected them. He knows everyone around here."

"Okay, that figures. I'll be back in about half an hour. I'll talk to him first, then I'll come to you. There's still plenty of daylight left. Thanks again. And congratulations!"

At that, the policeman ran back to the helicopter, and it took off, tilting towards the west, and headed off quickly in the direction of Picton.

"Nice people," Luise commented. "I only have one question. Where did the helicopter come from?"

"Yes, that's quite a mystery," said Jake. "But hang on, Luise. Isn't that your friend Doggy Woggy over there? You could ask him!"

Jake was only joking, but it was unquestionably their old fur seal friend who seemed to be waving to them. They waved back, and he dived off into the sea and headed off towards the point. As they watched him disappearing into the distance, they became aware of a kayak he was passing, which was heading their way. Jake took out his binoculars.

"It's Robert and his mum!"

They all ran down to the boathouse so they could meet them at the beach on the other side of the boat ramp. Robert threw Tom his rope, and Tom dragged the kayak up to the beach. They helped Robert and his mum Ray out of the kayak and moved up onto the bank where they could all sit on the grass. Robert and Ray were keen to know all the details of how the ambush had gone, and Robert, in particular, was delighted to hear that the point fieldsman throw had had such spectacular results, followed by the single-leg takedown maneuver, which he had seen Jake demonstrate so well.

"But we've got some questions too," said Jake. "Where did the police helicopter come from? Such brilliant timing! How did you manage to organize that?"

"Ah! Well, what I didn't tell you last time is that my husband is a policeman based in Picton. Henry —"

"Henry the Eighth?" Tom interjected.

"Yes, that's what they call him at the police station because he once made eight arrests in one day! Well, Robert has been keeping us informed on what's going on, so we had a chat with Ryan Scott about using his helipad at Milton Bay. He said he had met you all and knew about your concerns, and was very supportive. The police helicopter flew over from Picton about five o'clock and made its way up via

Kenepuru Sound and over Pope Bay to Milton Bay so no one this side of Snake Point would see it or hear it. They sat at Ryan Scott's helipad until they heard from us that your ambush had worked and you'd got him."

"Ah, you mean my text to Robert. 'Mission successful,'" said Luise.

"That's right, mission successful! And it was, too," said Ray. "But why have they got it in for you? That's pretty dangerous stuff, and it could have ended quite differently."

Luise explained that they were researchers looking at the plan for the future of mankind proposed by the German novelist Fontane, which involved a conflict-free world with people of all backgrounds working together in unison. Jake added that they were to have a major CNN interview in a few days and needed time to sort out their ideas, but there seemed to be people desperately opposed to their message and determined to stop them.

"Ah, like John Lennon, 'Imagine'…one of my favorite songs," said Ray. "I wonder who they represent? Who needs a world with war?"

Jake made it clear that they had no idea who they represented. "All they've told us is that we're naïve to think a peaceful world is in everyone's interests. They say that's definitely not in their interests. And Zach told me after I brought him down that he thought we were stupid, that the world can't survive without troops."

"I told him our New Zealand troops don't engage in war," Tom pointed out. "I said we use our troops for training and international peacekeeping."

"Quite right, but try to convince the military establishment that's the best way to go," said Ray. "Nationhood used to be defined by military power. That's changed here over the last generation or two, but it's not the case everywhere, not even in Australia. But I'm all for what you're doing. If you ever set up a movement of any sort, I'd like to be part of it. Seriously."

The conversation then moved on to the final member of the trio who had been trying to put an end to their activities.

"Pasty Face is taken care of, Beardy Weirdy is gone, but what about Cranky Lanky?" Tom asked. "The policeman I was talking to said he'd be interviewing him in a few minutes when he comes back on the police launch."

"Yes, he'll need to take a statement from you, too," said Ray. "What do you think, Robert?"

"You need to keep an eye on Cranky Lanky," said Robert. "I reckon he's up to no good. The three of them are working together. I've heard them talking, and he's involved with them, no doubt about that. I wouldn't trust him an inch."

"Well, I can deal with any 149-pounder like that

who happens to come our way," Jake grinned. "He reminds me of a guy I wrestled from Virginia Tech. No problem."

"And I can immobilize him with one of my patented point fieldsman throws," laughed Tom.

"Well, that's good to know, but I don't think they'll be falling into that trap again," Ray cautioned. "He might have something else up his sleeve."

"Let's keep in touch, then," said Robert. "If I see or hear anything, I'll let you know straight away."

"And we'll do the same, then!" Luise promised.

Ray said they had better get back to their place, as the police launch could arrive at any moment, and she was sure they would be wanting a statement from Robert and herself. She and Robert put on their life jackets, and once they were in, Tom and Jake pushed their kayak back into the water. With a cheery wave, they rowed off past the boatshed and back towards the point, disappearing from sight as they went around the rocks at the end of the beach.

Jake, Luise, and Tom thought they had better have something to eat before the police launch arrived. As Tom said, you don't disarm and immobilize an international criminal every day. They decided to have the sausages they had been saving up for a special occasion, along with fried potatoes and sliced peaches for dessert. Then they went back down to the jetty. It was still quite light, and Luise was hoping to see a dolphin or two. The dolphins did not oblige on this occasion, but she did see a stingray, which caused considerable excitement. They looked down towards the pohutukawa to see if there were any insects swarming, but it looked like the insects were finally returning to the trees for the night. Then they noticed the police launch moored next to the pohutukawa tree and concluded that they must have been interviewing Cranky Lanky. As they watched, two policemen came out from underneath the pohutukawa and climbed aboard the police launch, which headed out into the bay and towards them.

"Wait a moment," said Luise. "That is a swarm of insects! Look!" True enough, there was a cloud of what looked like dragonflies just above the pohutukawa. "Is Lake Stechlin trying to warn us again?"

The police launch pulled up at the jetty, and the two policemen who had talked to Tom earlier moored the launch and climbed up the ladder onto the wharf. They introduced themselves as Paul and John. Paul was the younger of the two. They took statements from all three, and like Ray, were curious as to why this American would resort to such extreme measures to try to stop them. Luise talked about their international research project, which was leading up to a major CNN interview on the Glass Mountains in Oklahoma, and Tom mentioned what Zach had told him — that someone had to stop them because the world couldn't survive without the military.

"Well, New Zealand troops haven't been involved in any wars for some time now," said John, "but I'll have to tell you that when we were sending troops off to Vietnam in the 1970s, I registered as a conscientious objector. So I'm all for what you're doing."

"Now, what's happening with the guy you just interviewed?" Tom asked. "Doug Clagon? We call him Cranky Lanky. How does he fit in?"

"Ha ha! Cranky Lanky! Well, we have just had an extensive interview with him. According to him, he has just been hosting Zach and Cortland as tourists. Paying guests. Put them up for a couple of nights. As far as he's concerned, they just wanted to experience the Marlborough Sounds, and he's been showing them around."

"Robert seems to think the three of them are working together somehow," said Jake.

"We don't have any indication that that's the case," Paul pointed out. "Doug's family's been associated with that bach for a number of years now."

"So he's simply going to be staying on there," said Tom. "No arrest?"

"That's right," Paul confirmed. "But if you observe anything untoward, let us know straight away. And keep in close touch with Henry and his family."

John and Paul then repeated their congratulations on a job well done, shook hands with Luise, Jake, and Tom, and asked them to drop in to see them at the Picton police station before they headed back to Wellington on the interislander. They climbed down the ladder from the jetty and reboarded the police launch, waving as they accelerated into mid-channel and made their way back to Picton.

It was now getting dark, and as the police launch faded into the distance, they could see it pass the flashing beacon off Dieffenbach Point at the entrance to Tory Channel. They were pleased with the outcome of their ambush and the support they had received from the police. But they were not happy that Doug had not been arrested. They remembered his combative behavior at Lake Stechlin, which had resulted in Luise's shoulder injury, thought of Robert's words that you could not trust him an inch and wondered what the night might bring. It was a quiet, thoughtful trio that walked back up the zigzag to the bach.

CHAPTER 14
Snake Point

"Tell you what, I'll spend the night outside in a tent," Tom suggested as they reached the top of the zigzag. "That way, I can listen for anything unusual. Probably best for me to do it because I know all the usual night noises around here. I think I know enough of them to be able to tell what they are."

"*Gute Idee*! That's a good idea," said Luise. "In that case, can I move into the bach? I'm not so keen to be in the cabin by myself with a Cranky Lanky prowling around."

They all agreed with this arrangement. Tom found a small pup tent in the room underneath the bach, and while Jake helped him pitch the tent, Luise brought her things across to the bach. Once the fly was up, Tom and Jake stood back and thought it looked pretty cozy. In fact, they wondered why they had not thought of camping outside earlier on. They found

an old mattress in the bach and put it on the floor of
the tent, and once Tom had put his sleeping bag and
pillow on the mattress, he had to admit to himself that
he was looking forward to sleeping there.

Jake made sure Tom had a decent flashlight
with him, as well as his phone. "You don't hear much
inside the bach, so you need to be able to call me or
message me. And if you're needing us at all, knock
on the door. Knock three times. Thanks! Have a good
night!"

"Knock three times if you want me," Tom
chuckled. "I remember that song. My dad used to
play it in the car. Good night!"

Tom then moved into the tent, zipped up the
insect screen, and got into his sleeping bag. Luise
called "*gute Nacht*" to Tom as she closed the door to
the bach.

Tom lay his head back on the pillow and
breathed in the fresh air. He had been coming to the
Marlborough Sounds every summer since he was
small and always enjoyed this experience of being
close to nature. He breathed out slowly and listened
carefully to the sounds around him. He could hear the
water lapping against the shore at the bottom of the
hill below him. He also knew that the soft padding
of the water would regularly change to the sound of
large waves for a few minutes as the wake from the
ferry made its way down the channel. Every now and

then, he could hear the screeching sound of wekas calling to each other across the bay. What he loved was the sound of the morepork, the native owl that would regularly call out a friendly "more pork" from the trees above him, as if to reassure him that everything was all right.

Tom dozed off, then woke up when he heard a rustling noise. He glanced at his watch. It had just gone midnight. There was that rustling noise again. Unzipping the insect screen, he poked his head through the front of the tent and, as he could not see anything unusual, decided to get out and have a look around. It was a beautifully clear night, and the lack of any pollution or competing light sources meant that the night sky was putting on a spectacular display. All the main constellations were clearly recognizable, and the Pot was particularly well defined, just above him. Tom recalled how disconcerting it was for him when he first looked at the night sky in Europe to discover that the Pot was upside down and called Orion's Belt. Further down, just above Arapawa Island on the other side of Queen Charlotte Sound, the Southern Cross was clearly visible.

Tom decided to sit on the step next to the tent for a while and look at the night sky, remembering that he used to sit on this step with his dad when he was small and that they would look for satellites. They would not go to bed until they had seen twenty satellites. That was fun because satellites could appear from anywhere and go in and out of view as they crossed the sky. Tom decided on this occasion he would not go back into the tent till he had seen five satellites. He focussed on the Pot, as he remembered seeing most satellites crossing there, or perhaps they were more visible in that area of the sky. Sure enough, it was not long before he saw a satellite come into view from the west, then another appeared from the north.

As he waited to see his third satellite, he heard a loud rustling noise right behind him. Tom jumped up and looked around. As he could not see anything in the moonlight, he turned on his flashlight. All was quiet. Then he heard the rustling again, coming from behind a bush. Focussing his flashlight at the bottom of the bush, he then became aware of a weka scrabbling away in the leaves under the bush, obviously looking for insects. Tom said hello to the weka and asked him to look out for any humans that might be approaching. The weka stared at him for a second and then resumed his search for insects as if to say he would bear his request in mind, but he had better things to do in the meantime.

Tom returned to his step and sat down, waiting for three more satellites before he went back to bed. It was not long before two satellites appeared in quick succession, proceeding in opposite directions through the Pot, and then he waited a few minutes for a fifth to appear, this time travelling from west to east through the Southern Cross constellation. He stood up to return to the tent and looked around, listening for any more noises. The water was lapping softly against the shore down below, but apart from that, there was only the noise of the weka behind him. Reassured, Tom said goodnight to the weka, which responded by scratching a bit more in the undergrowth, and Tom returned to the tent, zipped up the insect screen, got back into his sleeping bag, and dozed off.

Tom woke again a bit later to what sounded like some snuffling around his tent. Looking at his watch, he could see it was getting on to three o'clock, so he had been asleep for a couple of hours. Once he was out of his sleeping bag, he unzipped the screen and crawled out onto the grass. Looking around, he could not see anything unusual, but he listened carefully. There was the snuffling sound again. It seemed to be quite close and was coming from behind the shed in front of the bach. Had someone come up the track? Was someone hiding behind the shed? Cranky Lanky? Standing up, he tiptoed down the path to the other side of the shed, peered around the corner of the shed, and, turning on his torch, immediately found the culprit. Staring up at him, blinded by the light from the flashlight, was a possum. It had been feasting on the orange skins that they had thrown down the hill after lunch. Tom told it to please make a bit less noise with its snuffling so he could get back to sleep. Looking up at the sky, he could see that it was still brilliant with its clearly defined star clusters and noticed that the Pot had moved a lot further towards the ridge. Tom looked across the bay and over the channel, but, not seeing any signs of human activity, he decided it was safe to return to the tent and did so.

Tom dozed off to the reassuring sounds of the morepork calls echoing across the bay. When he woke up, it was to the chorus of the bellbirds from above him, around him and further down the valley. He remembered the dawn chorus so well from his childhood and was delighted to hear it again. He remembered how he had read that when Captain Cook first stopped at the Marlborough Sounds in 1770, he had described the dawn chorus as sounding like "small bells most exquisitely tuned," and his botanist, Joseph Banks, had written that it was "the most melodious wild music I have ever heard." Certainly, you could imagine that these were cathedral bells echoing down the valley. The bellbirds' call of melodious chimes was supplemented by the tuis, which often tried to imitate the bellbirds and even outdo them.

He opened up the front of the tent and looked over the bay to Arapawa Island, the top of which was starting to be illuminated by the red-orange rays of the rising sun. *Ah, the sounds*, he thought, crawled out of the tent, stretched, and contemplated the beautiful spectacle of the sparkling waters spread out in front of him. What a beautiful morning. *Nothing could happen on a morning like this*, he thought. *The danger must be over. Cranky Lanky must think it's too dangerous to be heading our way. Ah, good, now we can relax.*

He did hear what sounded like boots slipping on rocks, but he was determined not to get too worried by that. It must be those goats at it again. *They always start moving around in the early morning*, he thought. He went over to the promontory and looked down towards the jetty. Sure enough, his hunch was correct. On the next beach along from the jetty were the two goats he had chased when he had first arrived here. As if to confirm that it was them, one of them looked up and started bleating. Phew! Tom now felt he really could relax and was determined to just enjoy the surroundings. Becoming aware of a droning sound further downhill, he remembered that it was around this time that the insects started to move about and add their different-pitched buzzing to the early morning magic of the sounds; he imagined that these would be cicadas and dragonflies. Tom sat down and allowed all his senses to drink in the beauty of the surroundings.

Then he heard a loud screech. He jumped around and found it was a weka under the shrubs just above him—the same weka he had been talking to last night, he thought. The weka was not looking at him, though, but was staring directly down the bank to the sea below. What had he seen? Tom ran up the track to the toilet building. There was a spot just beyond this where he could see through the pine trees straight down to the beach. Yes! Someone was down there all right. A male, making his way through the rocks. It certainly looked like Cranky Lanky. And he was carrying something. A can. A petrol can? But there were no boats around there. He was up to no good, that was clear. Tom dashed back to the bach and knocked three times on the door.

CHAPTER 15

Jake opened the door almost immediately.

Tom put his finger to his lips as soon as the door opened, as he knew any conversation would be carried a long way in these conditions. "Shhh! He's on his way up the hill," he whispered.

"Who? Cranky Lanky?"

"Yes! And he's carrying a can of something. Looks like petrol."

"Okay! I'll be out in a second. Just need to get my jeans on."

"Right-oh. I'll be behind the shed."

Tom positioned himself so he could not be seen from further down the hill but could move around the shed closer to the track once he heard the intruder coming up the final bend from the left. Jake came down from the bach and stood right next to him so that they were both well out of sight.

"I reckon you should move out and surprise

him as soon as you hear him coming up that last bit of track," Jake hissed into his ear. "Try to grab the can off him. You should be able to get it off him if you leap out at him. The trick is to surprise him, just like Beardy last time. He obviously isn't expecting anyone to be outside the bach this early. He won't see the tent till he gets past the shed. And better if he thinks you're by yourself. Grab the can. Then I'll follow you and bring him down."

"But isn't it dangerous to grab a can of petrol? Especially if he's got a gas lighter or matches?"

"I'll be right behind you."

"Okay. Shh. I can hear him coming."

They listened intently. They could hear soft footsteps approaching from right to left just below them. They moved around to the right hand side of the shed, with their backs right up against the wall so that they could not be seen.

Tom was ready to pounce. He knew that timing was crucial. He could now hear footsteps coming closer to the shed. He decided to count to five. At the count of five, he leapt out from behind the shed onto the path below.

It was Cranky Lanky, all right, and he got such a shock at Tom's sudden appearance that he dropped the can, turned around, and started running back down the path. Tom ran after him, caught up with him, and tried to grab him around his neck. Cranky turned around, and just as he was raising his fist to punch Tom in the face, Jake appeared from behind Tom and grabbed Cranky's leg. Getting him off balance, Jake pushed forward, and Cranky fell backwards onto the ground. Jake then put all his upper body weight on Cranky's chest. Cranky flailed around with his legs, desperately trying to free himself, and tried to raise his back, but all in vain. He was pinned. If this was a wrestling dual, Jake thought, the referee would have awarded a fall, and he would have gotten six points for his team. His old friend Dylan Waters from the Bible Academy wrestling team would have approved. But this was a real life situation. Underneath him was someone who had been trying to set fire to the building he was sleeping in.

Jake shouted, "Leave him to me now, Tom. Go and grab the can. But watch out for fingerprints."

Tom snatched the can and ran back up the path. He discovered that Luise was already out of the bach, gingerly making her way down to the shed.

"We caught Cranky coming up the path with a can of petrol. There it is. Can you take it back to the bach? We must make sure it has his fingerprints on it, though, so just carry it by the upper wire handle."

"*Mein Gott*! What about his matches, though? Or a *Feuerzeug*? What's that in English? A lighter?" said Luise.

"A firelighter? Quite right! We have to be able

to prove he was going to set up a fire over here."

"But that has to have his fingerprints on it too. I'll just go and get the plastic gloves we use for washing up, and I'll get a tissue that we can put it in."

Luise returned to the bach while Tom ran back down to Jake.

"We have to find his matches or a lighter for evidence. Is there anything in his pockets?"

"I reckon there's something in his left pocket. Just next to my leg here. See what you can find."

Sure enough, Tom detected a hard metallic object in Cranky's pocket. Luise arrived with the plastic gloves and gave them to Tom. Jake put more weight on Cranky, though he seemed to have given up struggling. Tom extracted the object from Cranky's pocket, which did indeed turn out to be a cigarette lighter, and carefully put it into the tissue that Luise had in her hand.

"*Wunderbar*! I'll put this with the petrol can in the bach. Now we've got all the evidence, you stay where you are, and I'll call Robert and tell him what's been going on."

Luise was back five minutes later with the news that the police were on their way. Not in a helicopter this time, but in the police launch. She said she had called Robert, and Henry had contacted John and Paul, who were on a routine patrol of the Sounds. According to Robert's text, they would be there in ten minutes.

"Well, I'm not going anywhere, then," groaned Cranky. "How about getting that sweaty chest of yours off my neck?"

"I guess we can take some of the pressure off him now, Jake," said Tom. "Yes, let him sit up. We can take care of him if he tries to make another dash for it."

"Don't worry, I won't." Cranky wheezed under the weight of Jake's body. Jake moved his arm out from under Cranky's head, slowly moved backwards onto one knee, then jumped up and looked down at Cranky lying on the ground. The bout was over, he thought. He instinctively offered Cranky a hand up, which Cranky accepted, then they both sat down together in silence for a while, looking down over the bay.

"Jake, if you can take care of this man, Tom and I had better head down to the jetty to keep a lookout for the police launch," said Luise. "Could you just lock up the bach in the meantime, Tom?"

Tom and Luise left Jake with Cranky, knowing they were leaving him in good hands.

After a further silence, Jake decided it was time to ask an obvious question.

"Why did you do it?"

Cranky sat for a while looking out at sea, then answered. "Well, they said you were dangerous, and you had to be stopped."

"Who is they?"

"Cortland and Zach. They said you were crazy peaceniks out to disrupt the world order."

"Peaceniks?"

"Yes, pacifist nutcases."

"But we're not pacifists!"

"What are you then?"

"Much more basic than that. We are advocating the message in a nineteenth-century German novel by Fontane. It's all about overcoming the mentality of revenge. Rising above revenge. Stopping disputes before they become conflicts, stopping conflicts before they develop into war."

"So are you some sort of religious freaks then?"

"No. I was brought up as a Mennonite, but Tom and Luise aren't religious at all. Fontane's message was aimed at all beliefs and ethnicities, including Christians, atheists, and North American animists."

"What was this German trying to do, then?"

"He was living in a war-torn Europe and was trying to make people see sense. Get beyond revenge, he was saying. Rise above revenge. We need a world that is governed by common sense."

"What about the United Nations, then? Aren't they trying to stamp out war?"

"Well, they are doing their best, but is the message getting through? It was the United Nations administration that got us on this project. Fontane's message is a simple one that will work wonders if we can get it through to people."

"I don't know. It sounds good, but it's just not that simple, is it? What is common sense? People are going to dismiss you as peaceniks, just like Cortland and Zach."

"Well, that remains to be seen. In any case, if we hadn't caught you in time, we would have been goners."

At this, Tom rejoined them with the news that he had seen the police launch from further up the track by the bach. It had just passed the point and would be at the jetty in a couple of minutes. They could already hear the engine of the launch approaching. Tom and Jake decided it would be best to stay where they were, as they did not want to give Cranky an opportunity to escape on their way down to the launch. After all, Luise was down there, and she would be able to bring John and Paul up from the launch.

The police launch came into view as it passed the boathouse, and it pulled up at the jetty. Paul hopped out and moored it, and then John climbed out and greeted Luise. John and Paul exchanged a few words with Luise, and then Luise pointed up the hill towards the shed where Jake and Tom were waiting with Cranky. Paul and John waved to Jake and Tom, and they stood up and waved back. John and Paul then followed Luise up the path from the jetty. Jake and Tom lost sight of them once they crossed the lawn and moved up into the trees, but it was not long before they heard their footsteps approaching, just as they had heard Cranky coming up the last part of the zigzag just below them earlier that morning. Luise was the first to be seen, cautiously coming around the last bend, followed by John and Paul. Luise stepped aside and let them past. They briefly acknowledged Jake and Tom, and then John walked up to Cranky, who was still sitting on the bank with the others.

"Douglas Clagon?" Cranky nodded. "You are hereby arrested on a charge of attempted arson."

Paul then handcuffed him.

"Arson? You don't have a shred of evidence," Cranky protested.

"Oh, yes we do," Paul said. "John, I'll stay here while you go with Luise to collect the evidence."

Luise took John up to the bach and handed over the petrol can and lighter, explaining that she had taken extra care not to obscure any fingerprints. John thanked her, put the can and lighter into a fabric bag he had brought up for the purpose, and returned to the others.

John and Paul wasted no time walking Cranky back down the zigzag to the jetty, where they boarded the police launch. Tom helped release the mooring rope from the upright at the end of the jetty, and the launch moved off.

"Congratulations again, you three, on a job well done!" John called out. "Don't forget to drop in and see us again at the Picton Police Station if you can before you leave!"

As the launch moved out, Cranky turned around to face all three on the jetty.

"You won't be seeing any more of me for a while, but I'm sure the others will be organizing something once they get a chance. It's not over yet."

CHAPTER 16

As the police launch pulled out from the jetty, the trio waved at John and Paul, and they waved back, while Cranky just sat there looking bad-tempered and resentful.

"*Gott sei Dank*, thank goodness that's over," said Luise as they watched the launch move out into Queen Charlotte Sound and head back towards Picton. They gave a final wave as it moved off into the distance and out of sight beyond the boatshed. "But Tom, how did you know he was on his way? We didn't hear anything from Robert."

"Too early in the morning for him, probably. How did I know? I was out enjoying the dawn chorus when the weka that had already woken me just after midnight screeched at me so loudly I practically jumped out of my skin. The weka was looking straight down the bank to the sea below. I ran up to our lookout by the toilet, and I could see someone down below making his way through the rocks. It looked like Cranky, and he was carrying a can. That's what rang the alarm bells."

"So that's when you knocked?"

"Yes. At first, I thought maybe he was topping up the fuel tank on an outboard motor, but I couldn't see a dinghy anywhere. So I realized he was heading up here."

"And you both hid behind the shed?"

"Yes, we ambushed him just as he arrived at the shed."

"Ah, that's what I heard then. I was just coming down from the bach when you came up asking me to take the petrol can for evidence. You both did amazingly well. *Herzlichen Glückwunsch!* Congratulations!"

"Well, it was you that made sure we had the evidence — the can and the lighter — and had not compromised the fingerprints, and it was you that rang Robert. So it's the Glass Mountains Mission at its best!"

"Talking about the Glass Mountains Mission, have we got our manifesto sorted out now?" asked Jake. The others nodded. "If we have, then what's the story about our next stop? Because our CNN friends will be expecting us to be meeting them at the Glass Mountains over the next week or so. Remember, they wanted to meet us there for a launch of our manifesto in early January."

"Well, today's the second of January," said Tom. "Yesterday was New Year's Day, but we didn't notice because we had so much to do. Yesterday I asked my uncle Bill in Wellington to see if he might be able to book tickets for us from Auckland to Houston over the next few days. Tomorrow's Friday. I'll give him a ring now and see if he's had any luck."

Tom then phoned his uncle Bill, who said he had managed to get them reservations from Wellington to Oklahoma City the following day via Auckland and Houston. He suggested to Tom that it would be best for them to return to Wellington that day, as they would have a very early morning flight to Auckland the next morning to connect with the fourteen-hour flight to Houston. Tom contacted the local ferry service to see if they could get them to the two o'clock Interislander sailing to Wellington that afternoon. As it turned out, a service could collect them at midday.

The trio then decided to walk back up to the bach. It was now ten o'clock, and they needed a good hour to take down the tent, tidy up the bach and cabin, and pack up all their things for their trip back to Wellington. Once they had done that, they got back to the arrangements for their trip to Oklahoma. Jake emailed Ethan Lemaster to see if he could book them a cottage at the Sooner Suites on the University of Oklahoma Campus for five days from Friday the third to Wednesday the eighth of January. That would give them enough time to get over their jet lag and set up a time with CNN for the launch of their manifesto on the Glass Mountains. At the same time, Luise emailed Patrick from the CNN crew to see if they could meet up at the Glass Mountains sometime between the sixth and the eighth. She also asked Patrick whether the crew had contacted Judy Thorpe at the United Nations in New York in the meantime as planned. Tom texted Robert to tell him they would be on their way at midday, and Robert texted back that he and his mother Ray would be down at eleven-thirty to catch up on the latest before they left.

The trio locked up the bach and cabin, gathered up all their things, and headed back down to the jetty. As they walked across the lawn at the bottom of the zigzag track, a weka came out from behind the hydrangea and squeaked at them.

"Ah! That's the weka that woke me up last night and screeched so loud this morning when it saw Cranky approaching. Hello, Weka!"

At this, the weka strutted back behind the hydrangea and emerged with another weka and two chicks.

"So this is your wife and family? Pleased to meet you all!"

The four wekas strutted around as if they were putting on an athletics display, then squeaked at their enthralled audience. Luise and Jake took as many videos as they could before the wekas went back to fossick behind the hydrangea.

"It was as if they were wishing us a good trip back," said Jake.

"*Ja, schöne Tiere*! Nice animals!" Luise smiled. "Hey, let's go down to the jetty and see what's there."

The trio walked down to the end of the jetty and looked into the water. There were enough stingrays and jellyfish to keep them entertained for several minutes. Luise then took out her binoculars and trained them on the middle of the channel to see if there was any sign of dolphins. Over to the left, she could see quite a few ripples in the water, and she watched carefully. Yes, they were dolphins!

"Meine Delfine!" she shouted and jumped up and down, waving her arms around, hoping to attract their attention. And over they came. She counted seven dolphins, leaping up out of the water, diving back in again, and swimming around in circles just in front of her. It looked like each one was trying to catch her eye as it leapt up out of the water. Jake and Tom took videos of this amazing display, while Luise got as many selfies as she could with her dolphin friends. Then one of them took off to the right down to the boatshed and came back again, indicating it wanted to zoom off again in that direction.

"It wants a race down the beach!" said Tom,

running off down to the boatshed and along the beach on the other side. The dolphin followed him at great speed and then accompanied him all the way down the sandy beach to the first group of trees. It then leapt up and down and sped back out to sea. Tom looked around. He thought he saw something unusual behind one of the trees. He walked over and suddenly realized what it was.

"Come over here!" he yelled to the others. "It's Doggy Woggy!"

"Doggy Woggy!" cried Luise, and dashed down the jetty and across the lawn to the back of the boatshed, made her way between the water tank and the cliff over to the beach, clambered over the rocks, and ran over to join Tom by the trees. Jake followed her but took the longer route, around the front of the boatshed and under the slipway. He met up with Luise on her way up to the tree, where Tom was standing.

There he was, Luise's favorite fur seal, Doggy Woggy, with his brown eyes, pointed nose and long whiskers, looking quizzically at all three of them.

"*Mein Seelöwe!* My sea lion! Doggy Woggy!" Luise put out her hand to pat him, at which he raised his head, barked, and lifted up his flipper as if he wanted to shake hands. Then he flopped down and started moving off towards the sea, pulling himself along with his front flippers. Once he reached the sea, he dived in, turned around, so he was facing them and raised his front flipper again as if he was waving.

"What a lovely farewell!" said Luise. "I'd come back here any time. Here we're surrounded by friends."

"Well, we are when we have dealt with the dangerous humans," laughed Jake.

"Talking about humans, we'd better make our way back to the jetty so we can catch up with Robert and Ray," said Tom. "They'll be here any minute."

They walked back to the jetty and could see Robert and Ray were already on their way, just passing the pohutukawa in their kayak. They moved down to the beach to help them bring the kayak up past the rocks onto the shingle, where they both got out in a state of great excitement. Of course, they wanted to know exactly what had happened. Henry had already told them about the attempted arson. Robert was thrilled that Luise had called him so he could swing into action and get the police involved but felt bad that he had not noticed anything on this occasion.

"Luckily, I knew who Cranky was, so I knew who you were referring to when you rang me and said Tom and Jake had caught Cranky with a can of petrol and a lighter. Anyone else would have thought you had set a possum on fire!"

They all laughed. Then Tom explained it was the weka that had alerted him to someone approaching along the beach below, and when he saw it was Cranky carrying a petrol can, he woke up Jake and they hid behind the shed, ready to jump out at Cranky as soon as he appeared.

"Well, he obviously didn't think anyone would be sleeping in a tent and wasn't expecting you to be up so early in the morning," said Ray. "I know what you mean about the weka. The wekas around here are so friendly. A bit like having pet dogs. Our wekas always come out to welcome us as soon as we arrive. Lovely creatures."

"Yes, but they do like stealing things. You should see the collection of objects my weka has under his tree—including one of my sandals at one point!" Tom chuckled. "This one's a real friend, though. If it hadn't warned me, we wouldn't have had a chance."

They chatted for some time, then Ray looked at her watch and said they had better be off because the local ferry would be arriving soon to pick them up. Jake, Luise, and Tom thanked Robert and Ray for all their help, and Ray wished them all the best with their venture and said they would be very welcome to stay with them any time. As she and Robert were about to climb back into their kayak, she turned to the trio and added, "And don't forget, if you start any international movement, we want to be part of it!"

Robert and Ray rowed off in their kayak, and the trio waved furiously until the kayak disappeared from view as it passed behind the boatshed. As it came back into view, passing the pohutukawa tree further down the coast, Jake noticed the now-familiar sight of a large swarm of insects hovering just above the tree.

"Dragonflies again, Tom?" Jake asked.

"I think so. I wonder where they're heading this time?"

As they watched, the massive swarm of dragonflies started to move out from above the pohutukawa in the direction of the sea. They could hear the loud buzzing noise from where they were standing. Then some of the dragonflies started to depart from the dense cloud of insects and headed out towards the channel, forming a long line of dragonflies extending from the pohutukawa to halfway across the channel.

"Hey, this is just like what happened at Lake Stechlin!" Tom cried out. "The Atafu omen is back!"

"You betcha!" said Jake. "Let's just hope the evil spirits really are disappearing this time."

"They seem to be heading north, don't they, Tom? Up the channel?" Luise asked.

"They're heading to the northeast."

"Northeast. I wonder what that means?"

CHAPTER 17

As they were staring at the swarm of dragonflies moving off to the northeast, the local ferry appeared, making its way around the rocks from neighboring Spenser Bay. They waved, ran to collect their luggage from the lawn, and brought it to the end of the jetty as the ferry headed towards them. Tom helped the skipper with the mooring ropes, then followed Luise and Jake down the ladder onto the ferry. The three of them stood outside the cabin as the ferry reversed out into Queen Charlotte Sound, then started to make its way down towards Picton.

"The wekas are out!" Jake noticed as they started to turn towards Picton. Sure enough, the family of four wekas which had greeted them earlier had come out from behind the hydrangea and were now standing on the lawn, looking towards the boat. Then they started to ruffle their wings and prance around as if they were dancing. The trio applauded loudly and continued to do so until they lost sight of the wekas behind the boatshed. They passed the pohutukawa and then Robert's bach, where he and Ray had pulled up their kayak and were now out on the jetty. Both were waving energetically, Ray with a big towel, which they could see all the way down to the point. And then, as they passed the point and the entrance to the Bay of Many Coves, Luise let out a delighted shriek.

Just to the right of the boat's wake, a huge dolphin leapt out of the water, soared up into the air, seemed to be hovering into the air for a moment, and did a spectacular nose-dive back into the sea, leaving a plume of water behind it, which generated circles of its own waves and ripples. Then another smaller dolphin appeared, sliding out of the water, again to the right of the boat's wake, and slipping back into the sea.

"A dolphin! Two dolphins! Meine Delfine!"

All three of them gazed intently. It was as if the first dolphin had leapt up as high as possible to see who was on the boat and then sent the second one to say hello. As the boat now started to pick up speed, the first dolphin appeared again, much closer this time, again just to the right of the wake. Just behind it was the second dolphin, and they jumped out of the water in unison, then headed off to the right.

"Wow!" Jake yelled. "I think they were saying

goodbye to us!"

"*Wunderbar*! I've never seen anything like this before. Such friendly creatures, Jake! Dolphins, wekas, sea lions. We really are guests of nature here."

"And some of the humans are nice, too, Luise — Robert, Ray, John, Paul, Ryan."

"That's what I love about this place," said Tom. "The birds and sea creatures are so tame. And the people are so nice. Apart from the odd exception, of course, like Cranky! I like the dolphins too. As I told you last time, we had a group of them following us all the way to the point."

The ferry slowed down as they passed a line of ten kayaks, which disappeared into the distance, looking like a line of seagulls sitting on the water. Then it picked up speed as it swung into Ruakaka Bay, calling in to collect a visitor, who was fondly farewelled by a black Labrador, then moving back into the channel, passing Waikawa on the left, and heading straight into Picton Harbor. Tom, Luise, and Jake joined other passengers disembarking at the road-rail ferry terminal. They just had time to drop into the police station to bid a hearty farewell to John and Paul before boarding the large interislander ferry for Wellington. The ferry left as scheduled at 2.15 p.m., and half an hour later, as the ship started to turn into Tory Channel off Dieffenbach Point, all three headed to the port side of the ship to wave goodbye to Snake

Point.

"*Mein Gott*! Is it really only three days since we first saw Snake Point from this ship on our way over?" said Luise. "So much has happened since."

"I'll say. It feels like three months!" Tom laughed. "We got a lot done, though, eh, Jake? We finished our manifesto!"

"You betcha. And we managed to bring some criminals to justice at the same time."

"I'll never forget our time in Innisfree," Luise mused. "We did what we set out to do and had some real adventures on the way. But what I'll never forget is how kind everyone was around us when we really needed their support – and those lovely animals!"

They all took their final photos of Snake Point disappearing behind Arapawa Island as the ferry entered Tory Channel. They then went inside and found a cafeteria table next to a window with a good view of Tory Channel. Tom explained that he had just had a text from his uncle Bill to say that he would be collecting them from the ferry terminal in Wellington and taking them home to his place, so they could get a decent sleep before the early start in the morning. They would have to be up at 4.30 a.m. to catch the first flight to Auckland, which would then connect with the flight to Houston. Uncle Bill had also texted that there would be a surprise guest for dinner.

The Cook Strait crossing took about an hour,

and they were just passing Fitzroy Bay at the bottom of the North Island when Tom received another text. This time it was from George Aurisch. As they had not heard from Professor Aurisch for some time, there was great excitement.

"But what does that mean? It doesn't make any sense at all," Tom sighed. They all crowded around Tom's phone and read the text. *Meet you at 7. Royal Terrace 4 Bush Seat.*

"Oh well, at least he's not at the traffic lights this time," Jake laughed. "Sounds like luxury to me."

Luise was perplexed. "Last time, he did give us some idea as to where we were going to meet. At the traffic lights on the Pfingstberg. But a bush seat could be anywhere."

"'Royal 4 Bush Seat.' Is there anything royal around Wellington, Tom? A Royal Hotel or something?" Jake asked.

"Now, let me think. There is a royal golf club. And Professor Aurisch does play golf in Auckland. He probably has reciprocal membership. That's in Heretaunga."

"Isn't that where your uncle lives? Where we stayed last time?"

"Yes, that's right, Jake."

"Aha! Then I think we know now who the surprise guest is," Luise commented.

"So Professor Aurisch is wanting to meet us at

the Royal Wellington Golf Club. Now let me see if I can get up the golf course map on my phone. Ah yes, they have a Terrace Course. Where is hole four? Ah yes, here it is! Right on the boundary with Trentham Memorial Park."

"Isn't that where your uncle took us for a walk after he collected us from Wellington airport?"

"Yes, Jake, you're right. He lives right next to the park. But what's the bush seat?"

"Didn't your uncle take us through a forest in the park that he called a bush?" asked Luise.

"You're right! Barton's Bush! A big stand of native trees. Richard Barton was the first settler there. He kept the trees for future generations to enjoy. I remember Uncle Bill told us about that. So there must be a seat at Barton's Bush somewhere near the fourth hole. That'll be down by the stopbank. Shouldn't be too difficult to find."

It was now half-past four, and they could see houses appearing to the port side, slowly giving way to the first seaside suburbs of Wellington to come into view, which Tom said were Island Bay and Lyall Bay. It was not long before they passed Barrett Reef and entered Wellington Harbor. They stood at the vantage point at the rear of the ferry, watching it reverse into the interisland terminal.

By half-past five, they had disembarked and met up with Uncle Bill, who then drove them to his house by Trentham Memorial Park. They told him about the odd text they had received from Professor Aurisch, and he did not seem the least bit worried, which seemed to confirm that he was, in fact, the surprise guest coming to dinner that evening. He showed them to their rooms and suggested that if they were meeting Professor Aurisch at the area they had pinpointed, they would need to give themselves a quarter of an hour to get there.

At a quarter to seven, they set off, walking down Barton Road to the entrance of Trentham Memorial Park, crossed the bridge over the stream, passed the cricket ground, and walked alongside the athletics field down towards the river, keeping the golf course to their left.

"That's the fourth Terrace hole on the left," said Tom. "Over there on the right is Barton's Bush. If we are correct in our assumptions, then there should be a seat coming into view just behind these trees. And seeing it's nearly seven, let's hope Professor Aurisch is there."

Sure enough, as they walked past the last group of trees before the stopbank, a park bench came into view, and they recognized Professor Aurisch immediately. He glanced at his watch and grinned at them. "Exactly seven o'clock! *Deutsche Pünktlichkeit!* German punctuality all right. Just like last time in Potsdam." At that, he jumped up and shook hands with all three and invited them to sit down with him.

"This is a very popular meeting place. A great place to sit, too. I love this park. One of the best in the country. I've been reading about its history. Apparently, Richard Barton settled here in the 1840s, and he loved the native bush so much he was determined to keep it as a park," he said, pointing to the forest of tall native trees in front of them, to their right, and on the hill across the other side of the river. "Look at those magnificent totara trees. Right behind us is the Royal Wellington Golf Course. Did you manage to work that one out all right? I was hoping your uncle might be able to help, seeing he's a member of the Club."

Tom explained that he had looked up the golf course map on his phone, and they had managed to work it out from that.

"Yes, that's the fourth Terrace hole right behind us. The lake is further back. A really attractive course, with some native trees that would have been part of Barton's property. But look, great to see you all again. Tell me what you've been doing in the Sounds."

Professor Aurisch was horrified to hear about what had happened to them, especially Luise's dislocated shoulder, but added that he knew if anyone could deal with such a situation, they could—they were the ideal people for this mission.

"As Judy Thorpe said, you are an inspired

choice," he said. "If anyone can do it, you can. But you know you have to remain vigilant. There are all sorts of people in this world."

Jake then told Professor Aurisch how Cranky had referred to them as "crazy peaceniks."

"Peaceniks!" laughed Professor Aurisch. "I haven't heard that term for donkey's years! But you are much more than pacifists. What Fontane's about is something much more fundamental. You put it so well in that news item I saw on CNN. 'If mankind is to survive, we must get beyond the mentality of revenge.' Exactly! Fontane's ideal is of a considerate and tolerant entity governed by common sense. So much more than peaceniks! But I expect people like to simplify things. They probably overheard bits and pieces of what you were saying when you were being interviewed at Lake Stechlin. You need to make sure there are no misunderstandings at the manifesto launch that's coming up. Where exactly are you going to meet up with the CNN crew?"

"At the Glass Mountains," replied Jake. "That's where we're going to have the interview and release our manifesto."

"At the Glass Mountains? Oklahoma? How appropriate! Well, I'll be thinking of you. I'll be in touch with Ethan Lemaster—give him my best regards. And Judy Thorpe, too, of course. Let me know how the interview goes. Send me a selfie from the Glass Mountains if you can. Well, we'd better get moving. Did Bill tell you I'm invited to dinner?"

The trio told him they had managed to work that out from the various clues they had been given, and he laughed.

"Well, you'll need a decent dinner tonight to get you through the long journey awaiting you tomorrow. Auckland, Houston, Oklahoma City, and then on to the Glass Mountains. They are quite a distance from here, you know — twelve-thousand-four-hundred kilometers northeast from here."

"Northeast?" Luise asked.

"Yes, directly northeast from here. Why do you ask?"

CHAPTER 18

"Jake's here already," said Luise, and got up from the breakfast table where she and Tom were just finishing the maple and brown sugar oatmeal porridge and toasted English muffins they had raided from the Sooner Suites office. After their long flight from Auckland to Houston, the connecting flight to Oklahoma City had arrived on Friday afternoon, Oklahoma being seventeen hours behind New Zealand time. Jake's parents had met them at Will Rogers Airport and taken Luise and Tom to the Sooner Suites cottage reserved for them by Jake's history professor, Dr. Lemaster. They then took Jake home with them to Corn, leaving Luise and Tom to have a decent sleep and get over their jet lag.

Tom and Luise spent most of Saturday catching up on some sleep, and on Sunday, explored the University of Oklahoma campus. On Monday, they spent some time at the museum of art, where their attention had been caught, doubtless because of their appreciation of Jake's connection with wrestling, by Thomas Schindler's 1984 painting of two wrestlers. Although they read that the painting is commonly interpreted as the struggle between East and West Germany, Luise saw it as Jacob wrestling with the angel, with Jacob's ladder right behind him. When they had first met Judy Thorpe, the United Nations Secretary-General's Special Envoy for Conflict Resolution, who had provided so much support for their mission, she had described wrestling as a biblical sport, referring to the Genesis account of Jacob wrestling with the angel. Luise knew all about Jacob's ladder to Heaven from her research, as it comes up in Fontane's novel *Quitt*, and as far as she was concerned, Schindler's painting showed Jacob's ladder behind him. Her conclusion was that the road to success was full of challenges that needed to be overcome. And that applied particularly to their mission and to their own Jacob. Jake had quite literally wrestled their most dangerous opponent to the ground. She wondered what might be in store next? All these thoughts flashed through her mind as she opened the door.

"How are y'all? Sleep all right?"

"Ja, *wunderbar*, it's been nice and warm in here, and the Couch Cafeteria is even better than last time. Great food!"

"Had any key lime pie, Tom?"

"Your favorite! Yes, we had some last night in honor of you. It was delicious!"

"Getting a bit of exercise too?"

"Well, on Sunday, we explored the South Oval, had a look at the Bizzell Library and the Great Reading Room and walked around the McCasland Field House where you have your wrestling duals."

"And I had a talk with the local squirrels that had gathered around the bell tower at Collings Hall," Luise laughed.

"Yesterday, we went for a longer walk, down Timberdell Road and Chautaqua Avenue, past the Natural History Museum, and along Imhoff Road," said Tom. "Lots of people out jogging. We love all the open spaces."

"Then we went to the museum of art and saw a painting of you wrestling an angel."

"Wrestling an angel?"

"Well, I think that's what Schindler's painting is all about. Jacob wrestling with an angel."

"Oh yes. Genesis 32. Well, we might be wrestling with a few problems today. But let's hope it all goes smoothly. In any case, we'd better get moving because we are meeting the CNN crew at the top of Cathedral Mountain at eleven o'clock."

"Glass Mountains, here we come!" said Tom excitedly as they locked the door and got into Jake's car.

"Today, we'll go up Route 281 through Geary, on to Fairview on Route 60, then we'll turn down Route 412 to the Glass Mountains State Park."

"Didn't something happen on Route 412?" Luise asked as she got into the front seat.

"Yes, that's right, that's where my good friend Dylan Waters from the Bible Academy wrestling team was killed in a car crash last year. He's buried at the Pleasant View Mennonite churchyard we visited."

"I remember now. You told me he would have been so interested in our mission."

"Yes, I often say to myself I'm doing this for him."

"Is Route 412 a dangerous road?"

"Not really. But it can be quite narrow. It's only a two-laner. I think he was trying to overtake a truck and got into trouble."

"Well, let's say we're doing this launch in his honor."

"That's nice of you to suggest that, Luise."

They passed through the outer suburbs of Norman, headed west, then north, and it was not long before they reached Geary. They decided to stop at the First Mennonite Church on the main street of Geary so that they could see the foundation stone which mentioned Krehbiel, who had founded the church in 1897. This was the Krehbiel whom Fontane mentioned in his novel *Quitt*, set in Krehbiel's

Darlington Mennonite mission, and it was Krehbiel's letter that had sent them on their mission to uncover the secret message from Fontane that had been buried in the Glass Mountains, not to be opened until 2019, the bicentenary of Fontane's birth. Tom took a selfie of the three of them grouped around the foundation stone. They then continued on Route 60 through the town of Fairview and turned left at Orienta into Route 412.

"Glass Mountains, here we come!" Tom called out again as the first mesas associated with the Glass Mountains came into view. Then he noticed something. "Hey, hang on! Do you have dragonflies round here too, Jake? There's a big swarm of insects over there on the left."

"Yes, we do. That looks like dragonflies to me. Haven't seen anything like that here for ages. Is Lake Stechlin warning us again? Heading northeast from Snake Point?"

They were all peering at the swarm of dragonflies on their left when the blue Ford Mustang right behind them suddenly moved out and started to overtake. Then something strange happened. It stopped overtaking as it moved parallel to them and just stayed to their left, confining them to the right lane. Jake had to concentrate on the road, but Luise looked across at the driver.

"It's Pasty Face!"

"Pasty Face?" Tom shouted. "How did he get here? Can you drive with a broken leg?"

"Well, I expect you can if it's an automatic," said Jake. "But what is he doing here, and what the hell is he trying to do?"

Just as he said that, the Mustang started moving more to the left, on the other side of the road, but then swerved back to the right again as if Pasty Face was aiming to crash into Jake's door.

"He's trying to force us off the road, Jake!" Luise screamed.

"Well, he won't succeed. We're staying where we are. There's a bridge coming up."

The blue Mustang kept pace for a few seconds, then moved left again, over to the other side of the road, and stayed there for a while, again keeping pace with them. Then suddenly, it swerved to the right again, heading straight for Jake's door.

Jake slammed on the brakes. The Mustang kept going, cut straight past the front of their car, careered over the side of the road to the right, and bounced down a steep crevice at the approaches to the bridge.

Jake moved over to the side of the road and stopped.

"Are y'all okay?"

Luckily they all had their seat belts securely fastened, and apart from being in a bit of a state of shock from this sudden and unexpected attempt to push them off the road, they were all in one piece. Jake got out of the car and had a look down the steep slope to the stream. He could see from the tire marks that Pasty Face's Mustang had hurtled down the hillside, collecting some shrubs on the way, and had ended up with its nose stuck in the water. The motor was still running.

He came back to the car. "I don't want to go down there because he might have a gun. But I don't think he'll be able to get out with his broken leg. I'll call the Major County ambulance."

While he was talking on his cell phone, another car arrived from the other direction, did a U-turn, and parked in front of them. It was a white Dodge Challenger.

Luise instantly recognized the man who got out. "It's Brent Lehman, the Glass Mountains park ranger! I wonder if he'll recognize us."

He did. He walked up to Jake and shook his hand, and Luise and Tom got out to say hello.

"Hi, how are y'all? I heard the screech of brakes and thought I'd better come and investigate. What happened?"

"Well, someone tried to force us off the road when they were overtaking," Jake explained. "I braked, and the car cut in in front of us, couldn't correct itself, and careered down the slope to the right of the bridge and crashed into the stream. I called the

Major County ambulance. I said we were just one mile west of the intersection with Route 412. I hope I got that right."

"Yes, that's just about right. And Fairview's not far away, so they'll be here soon."

"We're pretty sure we know him," said Tom. "He's been following us around in Germany and New Zealand. Cortland Heller. He's got a broken leg."

"I'd better go down and see if he's okay, then," said Brent. "But hey, great to see you all again! I know about your CNN interview today. The Glass Mountain Conservancy has approved it. They told me to keep a lookout for you. Don't want anything to happen to you. So you three stay up here."

As they watched Brent making his way down the slippery slope, holding on to shrubs as he went down, they could hear the siren coming closer, and within two minutes, the ambulance pulled up behind their car. Three people got out of the ambulance. Luise recognized one of them immediately.

"Juliet! Juliet Skylor! Do you remember us, Juliet?"

"From last year? Doing research up on the Glass Mountains? And you rescued Brent Lehman from a rockfall? Yes! How are you all! But hang on, someone's trapped in a car down there."

They explained that Brent Lehman was investigating, and Juliet looked down the slope and could see that he was now on his way back up again.

"We've got time for a quick hug, then," she said.

There were hugs all around, and Juliet introduced them to her assistants, Preston and Jeremy. At that point, Brent Lehman reappeared and reported that the driver was trapped in the car because he had a broken leg in plaster and could not get out. Juliet sent Preston and Jeremy down with a stretcher.

Juliet then asked them what they were doing back in the Fairfield area, and they proceeded to tell her about the CNN interview about their research that was to take place at the top of Cathedral Mountain at eleven o'clock.

"Well, the entrance to the Glass Mountains is just five minutes away, and it's just gone a quarter past ten, so you'll still make it. We'd better wait for a minute, though. The sheriff's on his way, and he'll be wanting a statement from you."

Just then, another car pulled up behind the ambulance, and a woman hopped out who they all recognized.

"Josephine Mathers!" said Jake. "This is turning out to be a real reunion. What are you doing here?"

Josephine told them she was covering the Fairview Horse Show for the *Norman Transcript* and introduced them to her two editorial assistants from Norman, Carlisle and Kirsty. She explained that they both had equestrian backgrounds, and they were all just about to visit a local stud farm on their way back to Norman when they saw the ambulance.

"We know a bit about first aid from horse accidents, so we thought we'd better stop and see if anyone needed help," said Kirsty.

Josephine asked what Jake, Luise, and Tom were doing back in the area, and Jake was just about to tell her about the CNN interview when they heard a shout from down below. Juliet recognized it as Preston's voice.

"He's got a gun!"

CHAPTER 19

At that moment, the sheriff's car drew up behind Josephine's, and the sheriff hopped out. He ran over to Juliet and then realized he had seen the others before.

"Jake! And aren't these your friends you introduced me to last year when your study was broken into at Corn?"

"That's right. Luise and Tom, you remember Sherriff Mike Swift? But what are you doing here, Mike? You're based at Washita County."

"I still am. I'm relieving for the Major County sheriff for a few weeks while he's on leave. Great to see you all again! Now, tell me what's happened!"

Jake told him about how the Mustang had tried to force them off the road and had ended up down in the stream. Brent explained that the driver was trapped in the vehicle because he had a leg in plaster, and Juliet told him that her ambulance assistants

Preston and Jeremy had gone down to help but had just reported that the driver had a gun. Mike asked about possible motivation as to why he had tried to force them off the road, and Luise told him she had recognized him as the same man who had threatened them in Germany and had tried to ambush them in New Zealand. At Lake Stechlin in Germany, he had raised his fist at Jake, and his friend had thumped her in the shoulder and pushed her into a tree, with the result that she had ended up with a dislocated shoulder. When he confronted them in Germany, he had told them that he and his friend knew everything about them from the information they had found on the laptop that Kobe Wight had stolen from Jake's study. Mike Swift, of course, related to that immediately, as he had been responsible for Kobe Wight's arrest. Tom then went into the reasons for their return to the Glass Mountains and added that they were due on the top of Cathedral Mountain at eleven o'clock for their CNN interview.

"In that case, you'd better get moving. I can take care of this. I'll go down and get the gun off him. Then Preston and Jeremy can bring him up on their stretcher. Is that all right, Juliet?"

Juliet agreed that was a good course of action.

But in the meantime, Josephine had been consulting with her two editorial assistants, Kirsty and Carlisle, and they suggested to her that perhaps there might be time for a quick chat with the trio before they set off.

"If you're having an interview with CNN, it must be pretty important stuff," said Carlisle. "Have you got some material we could use? Then we could write it up in tomorrow's edition of the *Norman Transcript*."

"Good idea," Josephine agreed. "Have you got some sort of a press release?"

Jake went to the car and came back with a copy of their manifesto. Josephine glanced through it.

"Ah! Perfect for the mid-week front page!"

She showed it to Carlisle and Kirsty, who agreed wholeheartedly, and said they would work on it in the car so they could write it up as soon as they got back.

"Oh good," Tom chuckled. "That gives me a good excuse to go for an early run tomorrow on my Timberdell Road-Chautaqua Avenue-Imhoff Road circuit, so I can get a copy of the *Norman Transcript* from the 7-Eleven."

"Well, we haven't even made it to the Glass Mountains yet, so we'd better get moving now, don't you think, Jake?" said Luise.

"You betcha. Thanks, Josephine, Kirsty, Carlisle!"

Juliet came over from the top of the bank, and they thanked her as well. Then they all shook hands and wished each other the best. It was a fond farewell—everyone waved as the trio departed down the road in the direction of the Glass Mountains.

It was not long before they saw the large sign at the entrance to the state park and moved off the main highway into the parking lot. A large CNN van was already in evidence there, and they parked next to it, but when they got out, it was clear that there was no one in it, so they assumed the CNN crew had already made their way up the steep slopes to Cathedral Mountain to set up their equipment in advance.

"Well, we're lucky with the weather. Look at those colors," said Tom, and they all surveyed the stunning landscape before them, the shades of grey at the top of the promontory giving way to the bright red slopes dotted with dark green trees, down to the lush green of the grass below. They walked over to the beginning of the hiking track and looked up at the adjacent hill with horizontal rock layers on its bright orange slopes.

"Let's see if the sun's in the right place to reflect the selenite crystals," Jake commented as they proceeded down the track. As they moved towards the hill, it did start to sparkle back at them.

"*Wunderbar*," Luise beamed and took out her phone to take a selfie of herself and the others, with the reflecting glass slopes behind them.

Tom had a look. "Very nice! Let's send one of

these to Professor Aurisch."

"Oh, and here's the sign warning about snakes. Rattler Rules! We've moved from Snake Point to Snake Mountain!" laughed Tom.

They took some free souvenir selenite crystals for hikers from the basket at the base of the track—"For the whanau back home," as Tom put it—and proceeded up the steep hiking trail to a clearing which led them to the track up to the promontory. As they approached the large stand of trees at the top, they stopped to take in the beautiful view. Straight in front of them was a mesa with sparkling red slopes and further glossy mountains behind it, merging with rolling countryside in the distance.

"They do sparkle like jewels," said Luise. "Just like last time. Glittering mesas."

They proceeded past the group of trees, and there, as they had expected, was the CNN crew setting up their cameras.

"Well, hi! Hey, it's the Glass Mountains team!" Patrick McBryde recognized them immediately and came across to shake their hands. He was followed by Helen Harlowe.

"What a beautiful spot! Sparkling mountains. Glittering slopes. Never seen anything like it before. Like mirrors!" said Helen. "What makes it reflect like this?"

Jake explained that it was selenite crystals

embedded in the earth that reflected the sun. He said the gypsum strata in the form of selenite crystals and satin spar had been left behind by an inland sea. He added that the reflections were particularly striking after a bit of rain because the rain got rid of the red dust. Then when the sun shone on it them, they would act like spotlights. That was how they found Fontane's message, by exploring the spot where the spotlight reflections converged.

"So that's how the mountains got their name?"

"Yes. The story goes that one of the early explorers called it the Glass Mountains because of the way the sun was glistening off the slopes in the early morning. He had a Boston accent, and the cartographer thought he had said 'gloss.' That's why some people still call it the Gloss Mountains, but from what I've read, Glass Mountains is the correct version. It's been on official maps since 1873."

"You remember the other members of the team?" asked Patrick, taking them over to the others, who were busy setting up the cameras and microphones. "Keith Leighton, our technician, Christine Niven, our audio engineer, and Brian Duncan, the cameraman." There were handshakes all around. "So you got here all right? Any more trouble with those two guys that assaulted you back at Lake Stechlin?"

They proceeded to tell Patrick all about Pasty Face, Beardy Weirdy, and Cranky Lanky and how

Pasty Face had tried to force them off the road on the way there. Patrick praised them for their quick responses and common sense behavior and was pleased to hear that all three were now in the hands of the police. He added that they had received a very positive response to the CNN news item based around the interview with them at Lake Stechlin and said that viewers were obviously looking forward to the launch of the manifesto.

"By the way, did Christine and Keith manage to catch up with the strange phenomena we witnessed on Lake Stechlin?" asked Luise.

"No, it seems by the time they got there, it had all petered out, unfortunately," said Patrick. "They did get some good audio takes and drone shots of the lake, though. Now, back to the manifesto launch. You've got a hard copy of the manifesto you emailed to us? We've cleared it with Judy Thorpe at the United Nations. She's one hundred percent behind you. What we'll do is interview all three of you. Helen will go into the Fontane connection in the introduction and will interview you as a group, but in that interview, I'd like each of you to identify with one particular aspect of your manifesto. And then, for the final summary, I'd like each of you to come up with a very simple concept which epitomizes what you are setting out to achieve. Something that will appeal to our audience. I'll leave you for a couple of minutes to see what you can sort out while we work out the mechanics of exactly where we are going to be standing and what angle Keith wants the drone to be filming from."

Jake, Luise, and Tom sat down on the grass and had a good look through the manifesto. It did not take them long to find out the parts they identified with most.

"The bit I identify with most is the message from Obadja's sermon about exploring alternatives to conflict and war," said Jake. "Maybe it's my Mennonite background, but Romans 12:19 means so much to me. Forget about revenge. Leave revenge to God. We must get beyond that mentality of revenge. Rise above revenge! Revenge has led humankind into so many intolerable situations. We have to work together."

"Yes, and that applies to all aspects of life," agreed Tom. "All levels of interaction. In our families, in our workplace, in the clubs we belong to, in all the projects we undertake. What I like in particular is Fontane's ideal of a civilized state, a tolerant and considerate entity governed by common sense. No more divisiveness. We can overcome our differences and work together."

"What appeals to me most is the fact that although Obadja is the head of a Mennonite mission station, he accepts everyone into his community," Luise observed. "People of all ethnicities, racial backgrounds, and beliefs. In *Quitt,* he advocates a multi-lingual, multi-racial, multi-religious community as a model, which he hopes Europe and the world will follow so that everyone will work together."

"So Tom, I say we *have* to work together, you say we *can* work together, and Luise says we *will* all work together. That's the message we need to get across. If humankind and the world we live in are to survive, we must all work together. No more divisions, no more conflict, no more thoughts of revenge. Rise above revenge. Cooperation, collaboration is the key. We have to work together. Those are the key points we need to get across in the interview."

They called Helen and Patrick over and discussed these ideas with them. They agreed that that was a strong message that would come across well to the viewers and listeners.

"How about we move over to the spot where the beams of light converged last time you were up here, where you found Fontane's message?" Keith suggested. "I'll get a drone shot of you shaking hands with Helen at the top of Cathedral Mountain. Should look quite dramatic."

"Will we have to shake hands three times again?" Tom joked.

"Just once should do this time — let's see how it goes."

The trio moved to the spot where they had

discovered the box with Fontane's message. They waited for Keith's go-ahead as he set up his drone to take off and then maneuvered it into position just above them. At a signal from Keith, Helen emerged from behind the trees, walked up to the trio, and shook their hands. Keith suggested they should try it again from a different angle. "Just twice should do," he said. Christine then attached small microphones to their jackets, Brian set up the camera, and the interview itself began. It proceeded very much as they had planned, and everyone was pleased with the result.

Helen told them that for her, it was an inspiring interview. "You have a very strong message. Rise above revenge. You said that with such conviction, Jake! And what you said about common sense, Tom. And your comment, Luise, about everyone working together. If humankind and the world we live in are to survive, we must all work together. How absolutely true. I'll have to say it was a privilege to interview you."

Helen called Christine over to remove the microphones, and they were just walking back to rejoin the rest of the CNN crew when they heard Jake call out to them.

"Hey, look at this!"

They turned around, and to their amazement, discovered that Jake, Luise, and Tom were bathed in a shaft of light. They looked across the canyon and saw that the sun was reflecting so brightly from a spot at the top of the Lone Peak Mountain that it was impossible to look at it directly. Then another beam of light appeared from their right, from the slopes of Cathedral Mountain, aimed directly at them.

"The spotlights are converging on us!" Jake yelled. "Just like last year!"

CHAPTER 20

Keith ran over to them. "Wow! This will make an awesome shot! I realize at the summer solstice you had several beacons of light—was it five?—converging on the same spot. But just two is amazing! Just stay where you are, and I'll get the drone in the right place."

The rest of the crew was utterly transfixed by the beauty of what was unfolding before their eyes. Luise, Jake, and Tom stood looking down the valley between Cathedral Mountain and Lone Peak Mountain, bathed in the two shafts of sunlight reflecting across the valley and above them from what looked like huge selenite mirrors.

"Hey, you really are in the limelight now!" Brian yelled out to them, as Keith released the drone to take shots of them from various vantage points. As they stood there, another light from across the valley developed into a bright mirror-like reflection. They were now surrounded by beacons of bright reflected sunlight emanating from three different directions — two from the cliffs below the Lone Mountain ridge in front of them and one from the slopes of Cathedral Mountain to their right.

"This is phenomenal!" called out Patrick. "I've never seen anything like it before! Like three spotlights focussed just on you!"

"This is totally awesome!" said Christine.

"I can't wait to see this on screen," Helen remarked. "It'll be the most dramatic interview I've ever seen!"

Once the drone shots were done, Tom suggested the crew come over and join them in a number of group shots, as he wanted selfies "for the whanau back home — and Professor Aurisch, of course." Once these were done, the CNN team started packing up their gear, explaining that they needed to get to another interview at Oklahoma City before heading back to Atlanta. Jake, Luise, and Tom thanked them for their help and support because without them they would not have written the manifesto, which was now going to give them so much publicity. The CNN crew shook hands with the trio and wished them all the best and said they wished they could stay longer, as this was one of the most exciting assignments they had ever had. They then made their way back down the track.

Jake, Luise, and Tom decided to stay at the top of Cathedral Mountain for a while longer because they wanted to make the most of being bathed in reflected sunlight from three different directions. It was not long before the shafts of light from above them and across the valley began to fade as the sun started to move away. This allowed them to appreciate even more the magnificent view across forests and pastures to the blue mountains in the far distance. Just as they started to take panoramas and videos, they were joined by hawks circling overhead.

"The drone must have scared them off before," said Jake. "We've been standing still for too long. They must think we're fair game."

"They haven't read our manifesto," Tom joked. "Well, we'd better get moving before they start attacking."

Jake suggested that he could take them back to the Sooner Suites at the University of Oklahoma campus. Then perhaps they could celebrate with some key lime pie at the Couch Cafeteria. Tom and Luise were only too happy to agree, as they were getting hungry too. Jake said he would then head back to his parents' place in Corn and return to the Sooner Suites about nine the following morning because, by that time, they should have a good idea of the coverage given to their manifesto in the *Norman Transcript*. Tom said he planned to go on his morning run at seven, so he should be back with the local paper by eight. Jake said by that time, he would have the online version on his laptop, but there was nothing like seeing it in print.

***

As it turned out, Tom and Luise woke up a bit later than they had intended, and they were just about to eat breakfast at eight o'clock when there was a knock on the door.

"That's a bit early for Jake, isn't it?" Tom commented as he went to open the door. "Dr. Lemaster!"

It was none other than Jake's professor of history, Ethan Lemaster, whom they had met with Jake the last time they had stayed there. It was Ethan Lemaster who had arranged their stay at Sooner Suites.

"Hi, Tom! Hi, Luise! They told me in the office that you were staying at number fourteen. Look at this. I just got a copy and thought I'd better bring it around straight away. You *Norman Transcript* heroes have done it again. You're front-page news! Look at this! 'Strong message for divisive times: we must work together.'"

Tom and Luise invited Dr. Lemaster in for a cup of coffee, and they all sat around the breakfast table poring over the front page of the *Norman Transcript*.

Tom was thrilled with what he saw. "Wow,

this is great! Look at what they've written. We must get beyond the mentality of revenge. Rise above revenge; Fontane's ideal of a tolerant state, governed by common sense; We must overcome our differences and all work together, no matter what beliefs, racial, and ethnic backgrounds we may have; No more conflict, divisions; Collaboration is what it's all about; We must work together."

"And they refer to us as the Glass Mountains Mission," added Luise. "Look at the by-line. All three wrote it. Josephine Mathers, Carlisle Redwood, Kirsty Brook-Nelson. And they've made an excellent job of it. *Wunderbar!*"

"And won't Hans-Ulrich Menz and Hans von Dietermann be thrilled," said Dr. Lemaster. "This will really be something for the Fontane Archives in Potsdam to celebrate. And so soon after the bicentenary of Fontane's birth. You know, that was only ten days ago. Today's the eighth of January — Fontane was born on December 30, 1819."

Luise and Tom then proceeded to tell Dr. Lemaster about their adventures at Lake Stechlin, Snake Point, and on their way to the Glass Mountains. Dr. Lemaster said he had heard a bit about this from Professor Aurisch and was shocked to hear about their violent behavior and efforts made to silence them but was relieved that they had pulled through all right and that the three men responsible would now be behind bars.

"All's well that ends well. That CNN interview is going to give you a massive international audience. The Glass Mountains Mission will become a household word. You just wait and see. Now, that's the other thing I came to ask you about. Judy Thorpe called me yesterday to see how things are going. She's wanting to see you tomorrow afternoon at her office at the United Nations in New York. Do you think that's possible? She's put aside a two o'clock appointment for you."

"Does this still come under the United Nations STSM fund they set up for us?" Tom asked.

"Definitely. You couldn't expect students to pay for airfares and accommodation. And remember, your CNN interview was her idea. If you can make it she'll be delighted."

"Well, Jake will be here at nine," said Luise. "If he can make it, we certainly will, *nicht wahr*, Tom?"

Tom agreed wholeheartedly.

Dr. Lemaster smiled. "If I know anything about Jake, as soon as he hears about this he'll take you off to celebrate with some key lime pie at the Couch Cafeteria!"

***

"So the Oklahoma heroes are back!" Judy Thorpe grinned as she welcomed Jake, Luise, and Tom into her office. "The Glass Mountains Mission!

I hear you've made it back onto the front page of the local newspaper. I've been hearing all about you from George and Ethan. Not too good about your shoulder injury, Luise, and the way those idiots tried to stop you, but you would be the best people to deal with challenges like that. And at least they're now in the hands of the police."

She invited the trio to take a seat as she moved from behind her desk to her black sofa by the window overlooking the East River.

"Now, how did the CNN interview go? I know Patrick and Helen pretty well from the coverage they've given our United Nations stories. It was me that told them about the work you've been doing."

The trio told Judy Thorpe all about the interview and how the shafts of light merged on them as they stood at the summit of Cathedral Mountain.

"That will be visually so exciting," she remarked. "Can't wait to see the interview!"

She then asked if they had a copy of their manifesto with them. Jake gave her a copy, and she looked through it, reading out sections that seemed particularly relevant to her.

"Revenge has led humankind into so many intolerable situations. *Rise above revenge!* That's absolutely right. We must get rid of that revenge mentality. And you say Fontane advocates as his model for the world a multi-lingual, multi-racial, multi-religious international community. People working together from all ethnicities, racial backgrounds, and beliefs. Sounds like the New Zealand national anthem — 'Every creed and race.' No more divisiveness. Absolutely. *We must overcome our differences and all work together.* Yes! We have to work together."

She put down the manifesto and looked at the group earnestly. "You are absolutely right. If humankind is to survive and the world we live in is to have a chance, we must all work together. No more wars, no more divisions, no more thoughts of revenge. There is no room for division and conflict. Your message, Fontane's message, is such a strong and welcome one for the divisive times we live in. And working together applies just as much to keeping peace and avoiding war as it does to protecting the environment and dealing with pandemics. The reports we're starting to get from the World Health Organization about the Coronavirus disease outbreak are pretty alarming. The same principle applies. Common sense government, working together so we can come through together. We as humankind. You know, we're all one big team. A team of eight billion. We are constantly challenged by natural events, such as earthquakes, floods, pandemics, as well as other things which we ourselves create — environmental damage, climate change, conflict and war. But if we all work together as a team, we'll emerge stronger and more able to cope with the emergencies we face. The world will be a better place."

There was complete silence as the trio took in what Judy Thorpe had said. She looked at them intently one by one and then resumed.

"To summarize, if humankind is to survive, we must throw out all thoughts of revenge, conflict, and war. If the world is to survive, we must all work together. Work as a team—a team of eight billion. That's the message your Glass Mountains Mission must get across. And you will get a huge amount of support. Once that CNN interview is broadcast and gets onto YouTube, FaceBook, and Twitter, I predict your Glass Mountains Mission will get thousands of views and likes. Then it will really take off. I am proud of you and am proud to have been associated with you."

They all thanked her for her help and encouragement and said that they, for their part, were proud to have pioneered the Glass Mountains Mission. She told them to keep in touch and let her know straight away should they need any more support.

"I have the feeling the whole thing is going to take off by itself now, though. And I think future generations will be grateful to us."

After hearty handshakes, she accompanied

them to the front desk, and her assistant Brigitte Luciano escorted them to the lift. They waved to Judy Thorpe as the lift doors closed.

"Well, I think our mission has been a success," Tom pronounced.

"And if Judy Thorpe is right, there's a lot more to come," Luise agreed.

"I guess all we have to do now is keep a careful lookout for the Atafu omen," Tom ventured.

"Not likely to find any swarms of dragonflies around Times Square," said Jake.

"Come on, you guys! This calls for a celebration! Do you reckon they have any key lime pie in New York?"

James N. Bade, Professor Emeritus of German at the University of Auckland, lives in Wellington, New Zealand. When he's not busy reading and writing about novels by his favorite German authors or researching Germans in the Pacific, he enjoys supporting his wife and sons in their various pursuits, helping people as Justice of the Peace, running his own music radio station, driving his restored 1916 Dodge Roadster, and exploring landscapes.

www.ingramcontent.com/pod-product-compliance
Lightning Source LLC
Chambersburg PA
CBHW030323180626
46810CB00003B/1212